Off-Island

Marlene Hauser

Matador
9 Priory Business Park,
Wistow Road, Kibworth Beauchamp,
Leicestershire. LE8 0RX
Tel: 0116 279 2299
Email: books@troubador.co.uk
Web: www.troubador.co.uk/matador
Twitter: @matadorbooks

ISBN 978 1789014 495
British Library Cataloguing in Publication Data.
A catalogue record for this book is available from the British Library.

Printed on FSC accredited paper
Printed and bound in Great Britain by 4edge Limited
Typeset in 11pt Minion Pro by Troubador Publishing Ltd, Leicester, UK

Matador is an imprint of Troubador Publishing Ltd

To my family, for everything.

1

At half past seven on the evening of August 21, Krista Bourne decided she had had enough. She abandoned the ballet *barre* and her outraged teacher, Madame Chevalier, who shouted after her.

"Miss Bourne, if you'd rather be out in the rain then of course you should go. I am tired of your lack of commitment! You are taking my time, the other dancers' time, and what do you give in return? Nothing."

Krista looked back over her shoulder at her twenty wide-eyed classmates. Their arms and legs, for once not rigorously placed *en attitude*, dangled like the limbs of marionettes before the strings were twitched. The puppeteer gestured for them to continue with a sweep of her silver-headed walking cane and stalked after her disobedient pupil.

"You are not a dancer," she hissed. "You are always half somewhere else. *Always.*"

Krista nodded her head, aware there was some justice in this statement, and softly closed the door to the dressing room behind her. Madame Chevalier continued to speak undaunted.

"Now go, take the rest with you, and do not come back until you can bring me life. A full extension!" She beat the silver handle of her stick against the dressing-room door and waited for a response, a last gesture of defiance from the girl who had dared to walk out of her class without being dismissed. The only answer was silence. Madame abandoned Krista to her ingratitude and resumed her own place in front of the mirror.

Twenty soles brushed against the hardwood floor, toes pointed from the hip and held one count before brushing back. In the dressing room, Krista slipped the pins from her hair and allowed it to fall to her waist. She rummaged in the old flight bag she brought with her to every class for the cotton T-shirt and yoga pants she'd chosen to wear earlier in the afternoon, to combat the insufferable city heat. Tears rolled silently down her face. She disliked any attention directed at her, but this was the last time she would need to endure it. Really the last. She had been daydreaming at the *barre*, eyes turned to the skylight, watching the storm clouds massing overhead like half-wild animals, rearing and colliding with one another, dark and primordial, dwarfing the puny flashing marquee on the Gulf & Western building.

Madame Chevalier was right. Krista Bourne would rather smell rain, feel rain, taste rain, than stretch and discipline her reluctant body even one hour longer. Giddy from her own act of defiance, Krista dressed in a hurry, quickly brushing her hair and leaving it loose. Cool air rushed through the cotton clothing as she descended the steps from the fourth-floor studio. New York had been waiting for this thunderstorm since June. With her palm gliding lightly over the chipped banister, Krista secretly asked the storm to break when she was a block from home. *Let me feel the swelling, the wind, the pre-storm. Lose myself in the El Greco blue.* She tossed the flight bag over her shoulder, threw her blond hair back as if it were a mane, and stepped out in the long, turned-out stride of a dancer.

"Michael," she said aloud, her words drowned out by the evening traffic, the tired horns, and she quickened her step towards home, towards telling someone that things were changing. It all began last night with her dream.

She could not land. She was afraid to land, and yet it felt as if the choice were not really hers. She could not be flying under her own power, for she was bound, arms crossed at the heart, ankles shackled together, lips sealed. She was mute. In the distance was her mother, afraid to fly, and yet here she was, unable to land. Landing would mean taking form, taking color, taking shape. A personality. Landing was death, so she remained safe in her cocoon where every notion, every desire, was within conjuring distance. No law, no order, no others, only the motion pictures of a thousand different places and a thousand foreign names. A kaleidoscope of fireworks, the high-rolling rustle of beauty, the motion, color and light of insanity.

She stood upright, entombed; yet she seemed to fly invisible through the ages. Between sensory flights, she rested as pure concentrated energy, a beating heart, a steady pulse, housed in a canopic vessel in a dark chamber where dazzling, attenuated shards of light progressed slowly over the stone wall. The light frightened her. When she attempted to escape, to fly away, a wildly beating thing, the steady pulse rooted her to the vessel, to the chamber. The shards of light drew close. The closer they came, the clearer she could see her chamber, her crypt. But it was her heart she felt she must save from the light. If it were to shine on the vessel, penetrate the seal, she knew it would mean the end. Somehow it would change her forever. There would be no going back.

Then the light touched the vessel, cracked it… and she had been unable to scream. Michael woke her up, forcing her clenched arms away from her chest.

"Are you okay?"

"Egypt," she was finally able to say, "I dreamed of Egypt."

She did not mention the crypt-like room, the flight through time or the danger inherent in the light. She did not mention death. Michael said he could understand why she had dreamed of Egypt.

"You're wrapped tighter than a mummy," he said, and helped her unwind the sheets.

"My hero," she laughed, and sought refuge against his warm chest.

～

Krista walked towards the subway station at 59th Street, shuddering as she recalled the dream. A falafel vendor lolled against his stand, the flimsy yellow-and-red umbrella still upraised defiantly against the gathering storm, a threadbare fringe driven horizontal by the wind. Everyone seemed to relish the knowledge of the upcoming storm. A sitar player, a young man with a crew cut, smiled at Krista as she approached. She noted the odds and ends in his wicker donation basket. As she passed, she unzipped her bag and tossed him the pink ballet slippers. He nodded and she laughed, thinking things were changing fast.

Descending on the escalator, Krista momentarily considered walking home, or else taking the bus, anything so she could stay above ground and watch the storm roll in. But the train won out. It was faster, and if Krista had to choose between her redwood deck and high-backed wicker chair, or a walk down Broadway to the Village in a downpour, she would opt for home, for nudity beneath a familiar blue beach towel, and her three cats purring happily on her lap. She wanted to watch the parched oak tree in the courtyard welcome the deluge.

The train seemed to take forever. Krista missed the express at 42nd Street because her thoughts were elsewhere. They were on Ilsa, her grandmother, and what she might think if Krista were to stop dancing forever. It was she who had inspired her granddaughter to dance, to take up ballet for exercise and discipline, but also to seek freedom in movement.

"Like Isadora Duncan, see?" she enthused as together they pored over a sheaf of watercolors of the famous dancer. "Express yourself," Ilsa repeated and repeated.

Krista recalled many summer afternoons spent in Ilsa's small study, or else in the studio, usually lying against her grandmother's soft arm. It was she who discovered for the Bourne family that their youngest offspring had the odd habit of sleeping with her eyes open, especially after her father's death. But asking Ilsa Bourne her opinion of this evening's events was impossible. She had been dead for almost two years. Perhaps, Krista thought, her grandmother's death and not going to the Island, Martha's Vineyard, had made the heat these past two summers particularly unbearable. Krista sighed. She missed the woman who had always lived on the Island, no matter what the season, the woman who always seemed to have secrets and secret places, the woman whose iridescent paintings would never be seen by anyone so long as they remained in the garage, the storeroom and the boarded-up Island summer house. Her grandmother for some reason had never gone off-Island and, after she had died, it seemed wrong to remove the work she had accomplished there.

Krista bounded up the steps at the south end of the 14th Street subway stop. The sky, dark yet still slightly illuminated by the sun sliding to its rest beneath the horizon, reminded her of childhood nights when it was easy to believe the heavens were really one huge sapphire dome enclosing the captive earth. The rain began to fall. The wind blew in short gusts between bouts of near silence, strange on a city street. Krista stood for a few minutes at the corner of Greenwich and 12th Street. The theatre was closed, but the deli and the paper store were still open. In her plastic sandals she splashed like a child through the

6

widening puddles, thinking about dinner and her mother preaching in the Midwest. Krista hoped Michael had already eaten.

The rain continued to pour as she turned onto Bank Street. The slender dancer hugged her bag to her chest as if it might offer some protection from the deluge, then held it high above her head, over her already soaked hair. She mounted the steps of the brownstone two at a time and leaned on the buzzer marked "Michael Parks", over the buzzer marked "The Bourne Family", and over the buzzer marked "Charles Bourne, Sr." Michael buzzed her in from his apartment. Cosmos, the oldest and only male of Krista's three cats, met her on the landing. The first thunderclap drowned out the sound of her steps on the stairwell, and she slipped past Michael's closed door, heading for her own apartment.

The brownstone was once a single gracious residence. The Bourne family had occupied it for generations. It still belonged to her grandfather but now the building was divided into three separate apartments. Grandfather Bourne lived his quiet and somewhat mysterious life upstairs, except on the weekends when, until her death, he visited his wife, Ilsa, on the Island. His son's widow and daughter lived in the middle apartment. And the first floor recently had been rented, at Grandfather's suggestion, to Michael. No one had wondered at the old man's offer. If it seemed an odd thing to offer living space to a granddaughter's lover in his own home, and later to find him a position in the family firm, no one ever questioned Grandfather Bourne, who continued to come and go, in his strange, preoccupied way, mostly in the wee hours of the morning. From the patriarch of the Bourne family, nothing was unexpected, nothing was out of the ordinary.

Krista had her grandfather to thank for what she considered the most hideous name on any roster. Charles Bourne, in February of 1955, the month of Krista's birth, had served as a member of the General Energy team that transformed graphite into diamond. Hence, her name. Helen Bourne, Krista's mother, claimed she initially fought against it, then helplessly submitted to a hospital room full of well-wishing alchemists.

"I'm surprised," she often said, "that instead of Crystal they didn't name you Charcoal. I fought for Krista! Can you imagine being called Crystal, after a rock formation? That is what they wanted to call you – Crystal or Diamond. So enjoy Krista, and count your blessings."

Helen Bourne also claimed, whenever the conversation came around to birth, particularly Krista's, that she had wanted an abortion. She had not wanted to marry, not Charles Bourne, not anyone. If abortions had been legal then, she often told her daughter, if she had had the wherewithal to seek out an abortionist, she would have suffered anything. Instead she married and had the child, her only one. This Krista's mother told her when she first menstruated, when she became able to give birth herself, and the story had been told to her many times since. But Helen Bourne often added affectionately, "Despite it all, you're not half bad. Sometimes, I even like you."

In her apartment, Krista disrobed, dropping her clothes in the middle of the living-room floor on the Persian carpet. She picked up Cosmos and turned the answering machine to playback. Her mother's voice rasped, "It's a fraud, Kris. They send you out here to sign books for one reason only – so they can't be returned. I signed two hundred and fifty copies today. Can you imagine?

"Listen, Kris, tell Daddy Bourne I won't be taking the Nova Scotia trip but it was kind of him to offer. Oh, and if you want to get out of the City, take the car. You take the trip instead. D.B. won't mind." She laughed. "D.B., as we all know, probably won't notice the difference. The trip's been extended. I won't be back until mid-October. Any auditions?" The machine clicked and Helen's voice was cut off.

Krista opened the French windows to the deck. She tied the drapes back, and in her blue beach towel sat in the high-backed chair with Christmas on one arm and Allegro on the other. Cosmos purred in her lap. The wind picked up, the downpour intensified, the temperature plummeted. Except for street and house lights, the night turned pitch-black. In the three high walls of the apartment blocks surrounding the courtyard and the oak tree, shades were lifted and drawn at random. Dark figures here and there stayed looking out, as Krista did, at the storm. The discomfort of the heat lifted, the City seemed to sigh with relief. Krista sat perfectly still, not even noticing the silhouette of a neighbor waving to her, sharing the chilly pleasure of the overdue summer storm. She stroked Cosmos. An onlooker might almost think her asleep with her eyes open, or, as Madame Chevalier had said, might suppose her half somewhere else.

9

Now go, take the rest with you. Krista remembered the stinging words and pondered where she might go. To Daddy's ceiling? She closed her eyes. *A full extension?* She stretched out her legs, rotating the ankles, turning the leg out at the hip. She wanted to wake up… but then she wondered, from what?

At that moment, Krista experienced a hint of freedom – as if something had risen up from the cracked vessel she had seen in her dream. It moved, floated to the corner of the chamber where the light filtered in. It seemed to raise a long slender hand, pulling back a musty, heavy piece of canvas. Krista recognized her own hand. Behind the heavy curtain, she glimpsed the twilight from which she was being offered a star. She held her breath, clutched the cat close, feeling for its heart. *There are so many stars*, she thought, and then chose one.

She shivered. What a silly daydream. Wind buffeted the rain against the deck. The cats sprang away, running through the French doors. Krista returned to contemplating the star. What was that dream all about? Maybe nothing. She imagined a star breaking like water and herself stepping into the twilight, then dropping her hand, allowing the canvas to fall back behind her. Immediately, she found herself freezing.

"What do you want – to get pneumonia?" asked Michael, stepping onto the deck. He knelt down in front of Krista as he pulled the blue beach towel up around her shoulders.

"No," she answered, startled. "I lost track. I was thinking about that dream I had last night."

"Come to bed," he said, "you can finish it tonight."

"Don't be ridiculous."

"I'm not being ridiculous," he answered, stung by her dismissive tone.

"You are," she said softly, refusing to fight.

"Why didn't you come in downstairs?"

"Because I never sleep downstairs."

"I asked you to, remember, last night?" Michael's brown eyes were warm and pleading with her. "I feel awkward always sleeping in your old room, in your mother's apartment – the nursery even. Why didn't anyone paint over that ceiling after your father's death?" he asked. "I hate it. It gives me the creeps. When you were a baby, a child, it might have been a good idea but…"

"Leave it, Michael. The ceiling looks good at night. It's only by day that it looks bad, and who really looks at it then?"

"I do. I see it first thing, as soon as I wake up – the first thing."

"Keep your eyes closed, then. It's my bedroom. Always has been. And if you want to sleep with me, Mr. Parks…"

"And if I didn't?" he answered playfully.

Krista turned her back, tossed her arms up. Michael tackled her from behind, picked her up, and carried her to the room he detested. As he gently threw her onto the bed, her blue towel slid from the satin comforter and onto the floor.

"If you didn't, you wouldn't," she mumbled into the side of his neck. The luminescent stars Krista's father had painted and tacked to the ceiling of his daughter's nursery years ago glittered in the wavering light from the street. Through the rain and the wind-blown oak leaves, the tentative light seemed to quiver across the ceiling, and pulse, and intensify. And Krista was suddenly far away, swept up in a memory of the man who had once painted a sky for his daughter.

∼

The airplane engines droned as perspiration trickled down the side of her face. Her father's familiar voice said, "Nothing is as it seems. Take nothing for granted." She expanded as if weightless and disappeared. "Never trust your senses in the air. Watch your instruments." He was piloting the plane and she was playing her usual role of his favorite passenger. The glare of the sun through the windshield was overbearing. "There!" Charlie Bourne, Jr. pointed out for his young daughter. "Do you see Grandmother's house? Look for the apple tree."

The Island was not the same viewed from the sky as it was from the ground. Charlie turned the plane into a nosedive. The force was not sufficient to hold the slight young girl in her seat. She fell forward. He pulled up the stick. Blood drained from her face as he circled the house and the apple tree in one slow-moving, tight circle. "Do you see it? Do you see it, Kris?"

"Daddy," she answered, "Daddy… we're dying."

Charlie widened the plane's course and slowly lifted his daughter back to the center of the green canvas seat.

"No, Princess, that's only the sun, the hot sun. Daddy only pulled two Gs. Say two Gs, Krissie," he said as he attempted to explain to her the gravitational increase.

"Two Gs," she repeated as she saw Ilsa's apple tree, heavy with fruit. "Apple," she said, wanting to touch the tree. That would make her safe. The plane glided over the iridescent water. It sparkled in the shades of her grandmother's favorite watercolors – blue, lavender and sea-foam green. Charlie unbuttoned his daughter's white blouse, saying, "The sun will make you faint up here, Honey. The sun will make you faint."

She rolled her eyes at her father and repeated after him, "The sun will make you faint."

"Daddy's girl," he answered, and she crawled into his lap because there the seat did not billow beneath her. Her arms fit inside his, and she could do anything he asked.

"Fly us home, Little One, fly us home."

They landed then parked the blue-and-yellow-striped plane on the Island's short landing strip. Krista pretended to help anchor it to the ground. The metal hook slipped into the ground link. Amazingly, for a three-year-old, she knew a pilot's routine almost by heart. She knew the rudiments of her father's take-off procedure as well, and the following morning, when she followed Charlie to the garden gate, she knew where he was going and what he would be doing. He was going to test a new plane. Krista sensed his excitement and clutched at his flight suit as he left.

Pushing against the gate, first the dark-green frame, then the wire mesh, she called repeatedly after him. Finally, she forced the latch, which sent the small bells ringing. The summer nanny came after the child, and Charlie returned up the path. Kneeling, he kissed his daughter roughly on the forehead and gave her a tight hug.

"Listen," he said, "Daddy will be back soon. Wait for me."

Krista squirmed in her nanny's arms, trying once again to follow him. She pounded her fists against the white uniform. "Daddy!" she called after him.

"Go on now," the nanny called out, "she'll be fine."

Instead, Charlie stopped, came back up the path, put his flight bag down and retrieved his daughter from her nurse. He carried her patiently into the back garden where Ilsa was busy raking apples from the grass, preparing for the yardmen. He set the child down by the bucket under the drainpipe and pulled out a seashell.

"I want you to wash all the shells we found yesterday," he instructed his daughter. He placed the scalloped shell in her palm and folded her fingers over it. "Keep this safe until I come home."

He stood up, satisfied the child was sufficiently engrossed in her task. The bells on the gate rang again as he closed the latch and he waved back at his daughter. "Help Grandmother rake the apples. Wait for Daddy."

Charlie waved goodbye to his mother. Krista studied the inside of the wet shell. It glistened in her hand. "Yes, Daddy," she said, running to the gate, "I'll wait. I'll save the shell for you."

Two days later, Charlie Bourne died. His test plane exploded. Both the pilot and the navigator disappeared without a trace. In the New York City brownstone, the galaxy on Krista Bourne's ceiling remained unfinished. On the Island, there was a mock funeral with no body. Krista always remembered her father: the games they had played, his warm breath over her crib, his steadiness and reassurance in the bleached-out brilliance of a fragile cockpit. She preferred to believe Charlie Bourne had simply disappeared, fainting away under an overbearing, endless sun.

~

Whenever Krista slept with Michael, whenever they had sex, she remembered Charlie leaning over her crib. Whatever he had said to her then had drifted away, but the feeling of his warm, watchful presence remained with her. Krista loved her father. Charlie Bourne had asked her to wait for him, and she still did. She went out to greet him in the only way she knew how, in the secret space inside reserved just for him – what she saw as a cockpit in a clear blue sky.

Sexual excitement for Krista was a dazzling reverie. She pretended to be the dotted axis of some supernatural thing. She felt herself expanding as a vapor around a hot blue star or a planetary nebula around a blazing burnt-out shell. She ejected thin bursts of color like the remnants of an ever-widening circle of supernovae debris. She contracted. Pulsed. She took in a deep breath, and held still, searching for something in that white light.

Her breathing became harsh like her father's when he fought to bring the plane under control. She saw a thing recognizable as an apple tree in a yard. Earth from space. Daddy. She called out in silent fury to that arching thing: *Life enter here.* She was laid open, and drew in darkness. For one split second she was flooded, overcharged, bringing forth light.

~

Krista lay at peace in the room that had always been her nursery, the one with the stars on the unfinished ceiling. The rain stopped. The wind continued. In the courtyard, a few lights went on, and another few went off. Krista placed two fingers against her sternum. Her heart beat hard. She had conceived. She knew it instantly. A searing bit, an infusion of light, pierced her soul. It was like a switch thrown on, igniting in one moment every vein and artery. She imagined a circuitry overload, and wondered briefly about karma, about calling back the dead. She thought about Charlie.

"Life," she said, folding her hands over her abdomen.

"Krista?" Michael asked, as if calling from a great distance. She sat up in surprise. She had forgotten he was even there.

2

The following morning Krista awoke before Michael. She lay still, thinking about the ceiling, sadly eyeing the points of the five-armed stars peeling from their glitter-speckled surface. In the far right corner, a water stain, years old, spread in concentric iron-red waves, like a pebble tossed into the sky and frozen there. She touched Michael's hip. Maybe, she thought, the ceiling could be repainted a plain white. She would ask Helen, or better yet, Daddy Bourne. She nudged Cosmos, curled up at the foot of the bed, and turned on her side. The sun had not yet risen.

There would be no dance class for her today or tomorrow. Not ever again, she thought, as she rested her head on her arm. In a thousand years, she never would have guessed that one day she would wake up and not have to rise, pick out tights and a leotard, pull back her hair in a tight chignon. She would not have to race to make it to the studio on time, to find her balance and to strive endlessly for perfection. Auditions? She never really once auditioned. Directors saw her, invited her to dance for them, but even that was happening less, especially when they discovered she looked the part but could not deliver what they wanted most: vulnerability. More than one choreographer told her in vain: "Open up. Project!" When she did not, they demanded to know what bled her psychic energy. Psychic energy? What was that? Krista didn't have a clue.

She stretched deep into the covers, into the coolness at the far reaches of the bed. She worked her way back into sleep and towards dreaming. She laid a hand on her abdomen. Cosmos crept over her ankles and settled against her belly. She forced the cat away. *I am not pregnant.* The thought startled her almost as much as Cosmos's behavior. Usually he never sat on her lap or lay beside her unless coerced. *I am pregnant.* Perhaps, Krista thought, this is a sign.

"No," she said aloud, almost at once thinking of Deirdre, Mary and Justine.

The summer Krista turned nine, Ilsa Bourne had suggested her granddaughter study dance on the Island, just as she did all year in the City. Ilsa wanted more time with her, and she wanted Krista to meet the other girls who came over for the summer from the mainland, mostly from New York and Boston. Krista agreed because dancing was something she did every day, and because spending time with Ilsa was always fun. So in the afternoons, after a morning swim or ride with her grandmother, Krista would go with the other girls to the studio over the fire station. They danced together, dressed all alike in pink tights and black leotards.

The instructor would flutter her bird-like fingers over her emaciated chest as she spoke, and on Krista's first day directed her towards a pair of blond-haired twins who, unlike the other clusters of dancers, needed a third partner. The old dancer drummed her fingers against her prominent collarbones, impatient with her young students' delaying. Krista remembered the music: classical, oriental and jazz. She remembered the teacher's bright red lips, the incessant smoking and the diet colas always at her side. She never took her students beyond *pointe*, *tendu* and *glissade*. She believed dance was the ability to hear.

"Let the sound transport the body," she would say. "Become the rounds expressed in the ringing of a brass bell. The voice of Buddha."

Miss Catherine, as she was called, would declare in her sonorous voice, "Inner space is the beginning of any and all movement, and I want you to improvise, turn yourselves *inside out*. Breathe and dance. Show me that there is no difference between the *inside* and *outside*." She would then resume smoking, drawing hard on her thin, filtered cigarettes.

Giggling, the girls would dance, some hearing the music in their heads, their hearts, others only the wobbly 45 on the small phonograph. Each seemed to imitate the next, no one knowing where the gestures originated or with whom. All summer, the routine never changed. For two years, the routine never changed, never, until the day Mary danced out the plate-glass window and died, impaled on the prongs of the chain-link fence surrounding the fire station. Miss Catherine stopped teaching dance, and the remaining girls took up sailing or horseback riding.

Krista felt Michael stretch, not yet awake, on the far side of the bed. He reached for her in his sleep. She remained still, pretending to be asleep.

It was five thirty in the afternoon when Mary danced out the window. Miss Catherine's sermon regarding the *inside* had seemed exceedingly long and endlessly boring that day. As soon as she finished, Krista and her two partners stole to their coveted spot, the area directly in front of the plate glass. Mary discovered what she considered the best spot. She called it that because at five thirty, when the sun shone at just the right angle, both inside and outside could be seen at once. The girls could see the harbor, the cruisers, the sailboats and the fishermen coming in from the sea. Immediately in front of the fence they could see the tops of the trees. When the sun began to burnish the sea to a high gloss, when the glass was not yet dark, a dancer might perceive the faintest outline of her own body. This outline framed the *inside*, the girls supposed. Therefore, they concluded, the inside could clearly be viewed as the *outside*, a wonderful place full of trees, summer sun and water. All three girls agreed upon this dubious truth.

Mary discovered this same principle in almost every darkened glass, every surface capable of reflection – the shoe shop on Main Street, the ice-cream parlor on Wharf, and in her own extravagant bedroom windows. Any reflection became more than just a mirror image. Krista remembered giggling with them in front of the deli window once.

Mary's twin Deirdre asked, "What's inside if your eyes are closed?"

The girls pretended blindness, knocking into one another, the buildings and other pedestrians.

"Darkness," Mary said.

"Right," Deirdre agreed.

Krista did not. She was momentarily troubled by this girlish mischief. She did not see darkness. She saw her father's ceiling, a galactic expanse, a clear midnight blue where everything and anything was possible.

Mary continued with what seemed like playfulness. She looked into her sister's eyes, then Krista's eyes, and finally into her own. "What do you think the inside might be like if the outside were someone else's eyes?"

"What?" Deirdre shrieked as if the question were the most nonsensical she had ever heard. At once all three girls fell into fits of juvenile laughter and pretended to be spellbound.

Krista recalled Mary, the best dancer among them, turning faster and faster that particular day. She had never seen anyone's head whip around so quickly. She knew Mary was focused on the *inside* and the full sails in the harbor. She felt danger. The glare on the glass that afternoon had been particularly sharp. They had joked about needing sunglasses. Krista knew that while she and Deirdre recognized the window as an obvious boundary, Mary did not. Krista decided, then and there, her inside was her father's ceiling, nothing more and nothing less. Anything else might be harmful, dangerous, perhaps bringing death, as it had to Mary. And if Krista died, if she could not keep that magic sky alive, where else would that bright cockpit exist? How could she wait for Daddy? What if he should come back and find her gone? These thoughts she shared with no one. She never had. In a funny way, as she mulled the idea over and over, the older she became, the less she could really explain it to anyone – not even Grandmother Bourne with whom she felt she could share anything. Once she tried to share it with a classmate, who simply shrugged, and said, "Oh, nothing in that, it's just preverbal."

After Mary's death, dance classes were postponed for Krista until the end of the summer when she returned to the City. Grandfather Bourne, after hearing Ilsa tell her granddaughter: "You must get back on the horse and ride," bought the child a horse. Both Ilsa and Krista tried to tell D.B. that they were referring to dance but he would have none of it. He still felt another activity, like horseback riding, was entirely in order. So the horse he purchased and its successors were kept in the old stable behind the summer house. From that time, the summer they were nine, Deirdre and Krista became proficient equestrians, spending their summers riding, jumping and generally cavorting in the brush, never again mentioning to one another or anyone else notions of *inside* and *out*.

Michael grabbed Krista around the waist. He nudged her spine between her shoulder blades with his nose. Krista closed her eyes. She tried to hold on to her father's space. For the first time there, something seemed different, out of kilter, off center. Something, Krista felt, had penetrated the skies. She panicked, and yanked Michael's arms away from her.

"Don't touch me."

"What's wrong with you?" he asked. "You don't even have to dance today. You don't have to get up for the rest of your life."

"Don't—" she said, and threw back the comforter and the sheet and reached for the blue beach towel. Michael lunged, catching the corner of her towel, pulling her back towards him.

"Marry me," he said.

Krista stopped resisting, started to speak and then held still. Michael lay on his back, his head extending backwards off the bed and hanging down. He looked at her from his upside-down position with his blond curls falling away from his face. Krista covered herself.

"Some jokes," she said, "are not funny."

"Jokes?" he questioned.

"Jokes."

"Well, someday," he answered lightly, "I might just be serious."

"I'm pregnant," she told him.

"No." He rolled back on the bed so he could look at her properly.

"Yes."

"When?"

"Last night."

"Krista, don't be so dramatic."

"I'm not being dramatic."

"But how can you know?"

"I felt it for a split second. New life."

"That's impossible," he told her, frowning.

"I asked for it."

"For what?"

"Life."

"So marry me."

"Don't be stupid."

"Okay. I won't ask you again."

Michael jumped from the bed and raced Krista to the bathroom. From the shower, she listened to him sing. He sang every morning. He took such pleasure in life, she thought as she shook out the sheets, the comforter and the beach towel. From the bathroom, he shouted,

"You know what? I am going to repaint that ceiling myself."

"Okay, okay," she said, not really paying attention.

"Every time I sleep with you," he shouted again, "I get this ridiculous glitter all over my legs and everything else. How long do you think it can possibly continue to rain down?"

"Until the whole sky caves in," Krista answered from the kitchen as she placed two mugs in the microwave.

"Hey, Kris, you can't be pregnant," he said as an afterthought. "You were using your diaphragm."

"Failure rate," she told him glibly, "is four percent."

"What is that? A chance in a million?"

"I don't know, and won't for another three weeks. Unless you want me to take a blood test. Do you?"

"No," he said as she stepped into the shower with him. She shampooed his hair. Then he picked up his pace, finishing in the shower, drying himself, grabbing his clothes and peeking out the door, looking both ways before descending the stairs.

"Put something on," Krista called after him in a low voice. "Someday you're going to get caught."

"By whom?" he asked, looking over his shoulder.

"D.B.," she answered.

"You think he doesn't know already?"

～

Krista's day was slow, pleasant. She strolled, telling herself she was on vacation, for the first time in ages, not dancing. She walked around the Village, sat in Washington Square Park, fed pigeons and drank too many cappuccinos. *What if…* she asked herself, the pigeons and the summer sky. *What if I am pregnant?* She scrambled the features of her potential child – straight blond hair, Michael's brown eyes, slender palms, long fingers, male, female, tall, short, curly hair, blue eyes. Sometimes she could see it. She touched her abdomen, smiled and daydreamed.

Whenever she found herself reading a dance poster, a thing that had become second nature to her, she stopped and reminded herself that she was no longer dancing. Maybe all of this was meant to happen. It was fate. Fate that Madame Chevalier should excuse her permanently from class, that she should be pregnant now. A simple twist of fate, nothing more and nothing less. She continued walking, letting her mind drift and wander as it seldom had due to her class schedule and because before now she had always fled from anything that might take her away from her primary duty: to wait. Preverbal, she sighed to herself, recalling her classmate. Preverbal – what was that anyway?

Krista trailed one woman, then others – the ones pushing baby carriages. She thought she could spot the mother from the nanny, and guessed correctly the identity of a famous grandmother posing as a nurse. Pregnant women walked differently, she thought. They seemed less preoccupied by any awareness of self, all their attention fixed elsewhere. Krista became newly sensitized to the existence of babies all around her. Did these specialist shops spring up overnight? She noticed window displays of pastel clothes, toys of every kind, foods she had known all her life – Gerber's, Heinz – child-sized beds, lamps, desks and chests full of miniature drawers. Whole stores, she saw, amazed, were devoted to them. She took notice of schools tucked away on side streets. Windows were covered with runaway sweet-potato vines and children's handprints, cut from blue construction paper and covered in foil stars. The schools had wonderful names: Sunglow Day School, Country Lane, and The Olde Schoolhouse. Krista stole glances inside and imagined how in a month the coat racks would be overloaded with sweaters, lunch pails and stray rubber boots. She fantasized the growth of her child. *If she were pregnant.*

She daydreamed about Justine, Deirdre's baby. Krista remembered her mother going with her to visit Deirdre in the hospital, the day after the child was born. Krista remembered her friend holding the newborn girl, wrapped in a pink blanket. She had uncurled each finger and counted each one of Justine's toes. She described the moment when she saw her daughter's head. She would not relinquish Justine to any of her admirers. Lovingly, she asked repeatedly, "Doesn't she look just like Mary?"

No one disagreed. Did she want Justine to be her twin? Though Krista did think the child looked like Mary. When they left, she asked her mother, "If I had a child, do you think it would look like Daddy?"

"No," Helen said brusquely. "A new life is not a replacement for an old one. Your father is dead. Mary is dead. Deirdre is playing at keeping her alive."

Krista crossed the street and wandered towards the piers. She liked seeing the water. It made her think of Ilsa, even if the brownish New York water would never match the brilliant violet and sea-coast green of her grandmother's watercolors. As she stepped off the curb, a taxi swerved in her direction to avoid a hot-dog vendor moving his cart. A bicycle messenger barely made the narrowing gap between the silver box belonging to the vendor and an ambulance turning towards St Vincent's Hospital. Krista put her hands protectively over her abdomen as the taxi veered in her direction. It was instinctual. She did not have time to turn away. The cab grazed her knuckles. She stared at the driver. Then she heard the siren, which must have been screaming for several blocks.

"Lady," the cabbie hollered, "wake up!"

Krista stood frozen. She was frightened, not for herself, but for her baby. She crossed the street and walked away quickly. She started to run towards home. Her knuckles burned. *What if I were pregnant?* She unlocked the front door. She started crying as she let herself into Michael's apartment. She picked up a book, tried to read, sipped from a bottle of water that stood by the empty fireplace. *If I am pregnant.* She put the book down. *I could have been hit.*

She had been daydreaming. She had not heard the siren. Madame Chevalier's voice echoed in her mind. She heard the cane handle beat against the dressing-room door. *A full extension, a body with life.* She closed her eyes, sitting with the blinds drawn, the air conditioner on high and humming. Upstairs the phone was ringing. *I am not pregnant.* She felt disoriented. She felt lost, and yet, at the same time, buoyed up. She felt new life quickening inside her.

Krista imagined Michael as a husband and father. He always joked about it. She could not picture him in those roles. She only saw his mannish beauty. Over two years ago she went with another dance student to Central Park, to the annual bicycle race. They spread a blanket on the ground for themselves and popped the cork on a bottle of champagne, making toasts and eating grapes. Who ever had time off? Both girls wore their hair loose, and long cotton skirts. They watched the cyclists take their turns for the speed trials. Krista did not pay attention until Michael rushed past.

She pointed. "Look at him," she told her friend.

The two girls watched, considered.

"Careful," her companion warned Krista.

"Careful? He's beautiful."

"Tell him then, after the race."

"Tell him what?"

"That he cycled a good race."

"Here he comes again." Krista shifted her weight, and rose to her knees. "He's going to win! I can't believe it. Have you ever seen someone who looks exactly the way you've always dreamed he would look?"

"You mean the big *he*?"

"The *one* you're supposed to fall in love with."

"No."

"I think I will tell him…"

"Tell him what?"

"That he cycled a good race."

The girls smoothed their skirts, walked towards the finish line. Krista handed the stranger a glass of warm champagne. He did not, after all, finish first, coming in third eventually. He didn't seem to mind. Krista introduced herself. They exchanged numbers. Michael was whisked away, but true to his word, he did telephone the next day. That was what she remembered. Since then, it seemed he had always been there – tall, blond, dark-eyed, athletic. He would be reproducible, she thought. *If I am pregnant.*

~

For three weeks, Krista spent her days in the same fashion. She took long walks, watched colors become brighter and felt sound as something that assailed her. She almost cried when she saw a stray wildflower growing up from a crack in a pockmarked sidewalk. She protected herself from noises – subways, horns – and tried to choose carefully when she read a menu, something telling her to eat for two. *If I am pregnant.*

She never returned to the nursery after the night she felt she conceived. She made a pretense of allowing Michael to think it was because he had asked her to sleep downstairs and because he disliked sleeping in the nursery. The truth was she feared sleeping again under the ceiling her father had painted. Something had changed there. During the daytime she oscillated between thinking she was pregnant, knowing she was pregnant and then knowing absolutely that she was not. When she found herself considering what she might do if a pregnancy test read positive, she distracted herself immediately. She believed that if she started to think such things, it meant she really knew she was pregnant. *I am not pregnant*, Krista would remind herself.

Sometimes she would know for sure, especially when she awoke from a recurrent dream that troubled her for almost the whole waiting period. In the dream, on a solid, marble table, she became a sculptress, taking great care with her vision. The material she worked with was both solid and pliable. It seemed to have a heartbeat and emanated a soft light. She worked vigorously and playfully. She fashioned a face – high cheekbones, long nose, smooth jaw. The spine she played like a tiny keyboard. There were a poet's hands, a curving dimpled rump. Beyond lay a magnificent landscape, a place she had never been. Then she would awake in terror, feeling she had been tricked. There was no heartbeat or pliable stuff. There was only Michael's blank ceiling and his bare back.

Krista would touch her sleeping bedfellow, then get up and go to the window. She would stand with her arms crossed over her chest, looking at the brownstones across the street, the street itself, and the twilight she found more familiar than daylight on the street where she had lived all her life. Her breasts hurt. The nipples were sore. They were swelling. But maybe, she hoped, it was only from imminent menstruation. She tested the muscle above her pubic bone. It had toughened. This was a sign she recalled Deirdre describing. But didn't all dancers have especially well-toned muscles?

At the window she peeked through the blinds. She watched an old man hobble down the street. He stopped at two aluminum trash cans and began to rummage. Krista felt pity for him. Michael turned over in his sleep. She wept. None of this had been planned. She had not asked for any of it, she told herself. She did not ask for a baby. Did she? *Life enter here.* No, she told herself, she did not have that kind of power. Something else was controlling her. Quite suddenly, she knew what she would do if the test proved to be positive. She would have an abortion. It was as simple as that. She would do it right away. She would find a good doctor. It would be safe. Abortions were legal. There would be nothing to endanger the time when her situation was better, when the decision to have a child was planned, when it was not an obscure, bolt-from-the-blue twist of fate. *Life enter here.* Was she that powerful?

She realized for the first time how much she cared for life and how responsible she wanted to be as a mother. She wanted to be a parent who was fully committed and present. Her child would not be the extension of a fantasy, a roll of the dice. Her child would be someone planned, anticipated, truly wanted. Maybe it would be with Michael, and maybe it would not. Did she even know him? This child had come about purely because of the rain. Krista cried because being pregnant made her realize how much more than anything else in the world – more than a career, a way to prove herself to her mother – she did want a child, children. One day, when it felt right. She wanted a baby to love the way her father had loved her. But this was the wrong time. A woman could know it was the wrong time, or the wrong reason. Couldn't she know that, in just the same way she knew whether she had conceived or not? That split second. Krista wanted a child. She did want to create life, but the time and the circumstances now were not right. Krista knew she was not yet ready to be a mother, the guide and compass to a new human being.

She crawled back into bed, curling around Michael, pulling his head to her chest. She kissed the top of his head. He worked his body towards hers, mumbling, half asleep.

"What are you doing up?"

"Nothing," she said, "thinking."

"Thinking?" he said. "Not my little dreamer."

"That's right," she said, hushing him back to sleep. She held him securely, as if he were the baby she was about to give up.

She lay holding him as she recognized for the first time what women – mothers – had always had the option to do. They could, like gods, give life or take it away. Did it even matter whether or not it was legalized? This was a power no senate could legislate for. Means would always be found. Biology was not a process of law. The feeling ran so deep, so primordial, so original. She knew she could not share her pain, her responsibility.

"God," she pleaded, "I do not want to be pregnant. I do not want to have to make this decision. I do not want to cut this beautiful being out of my life. Please help me."

Krista still hoped the test would be negative. She wished the past few weeks would all have been the fault of her runaway imagination. She begged God to let the pregnancy test be negative, and promised to never again play with the power she had been given. How could she not have known, not understood? She wept. *I can create life.* She recalled that instant surge of light. The moment of conception was indelibly written in her heart and mind. Who, she thought, had separated sex from producing life?

∼

The early pregnancy test kit was a miniature lab; a little clear plastic support for the small test tube, including a mirror, so as to see the results at the bottom without touching the tube itself, a plastic vial with purified water, a dropper with a black squeeze tube that matched the black stopper in the test tube, all fitted over with a neat, clear plastic lid, which could also hold the urine needed for the test.

On the ninth day after Krista's period refused to begin, early on a Sunday morning, Michael suggested taking the test. He placed the kit on his dining-room table, reading the directions aloud to Krista, who remained in bed.

"HGC... that's the hormone you have present in your body, Kris. You know what it is? This is real scientific, you know. Did I ever tell you I wanted to be a doctor once? I loved bio lab… even the rats in zoology. There's something about white coats and clear plastic tubes, blood, veins, arteries. I saw a corpse once, in New Haven. My cousin snuck me into the anatomy lab. I saw this leg, an old man's yellow leg, and this guy was working on it, cutting away at layers, pulling at the fat…"

Michael walked into the bedroom and sat on the edge of the mattress.

"The fellow who was cutting away happened to be the lab professor, and he looked a little irked that he had been interrupted. But my cousin just said, "Hi, Doctor, this is Michael Parks, he's a first-year student at Columbia." After that I had the grand tour. There wasn't a thing I didn't see, even the fetuses. You know, Kris, there's a real thing called a Cyclops baby. They're born with one eye, right in the middle of their forehead." He crossed his legs, reflecting on the display case he once saw outside the anatomy lab at Yale.

Krista looked up at him. "Michael, what are you doing?"

"I'm waiting for you."

"For what?"

"Your urine." He handed her the square plastic combination lid and specimen container.

"So why are you talking about Cyclops babies?"

"Because I saw them once. Sorry… guess I'm nervous." He trailed her to the bathroom, where she closed the door. "Should I go out," he asked, "and start over?"

She laughed. "You can't start over. We just go on."

"Hey," he banged on the door, "lighten up, will you? You know, it could be worse."

"Yeah, I know," she said. "I could have one eye."

"Or one arm."

"Or no arms. Or..."

"No urine. What about that?"

Krista came out of the bathroom wearing Michael's silk shirt. She handed him the specimen. "No such luck, Dr. Parks. There's extra in case you miss something the first time around." She went back to bed.

"You are too kind!"

"Michael," she called from the bedroom, "I talked to a doctor on Friday, a Dr. Blackwell on Madison, near 73rd Street. He's got a good reputation as an obstetrician and for... anyway, he said he'd perform the abortion."

Michael was not paying attention to Krista as he removed the glass test tube. He practiced filling and emptying the dropper until he had no trouble delivering three drops accurately. He filled the dropper again. Then, holding it vertical, he carefully let three drops fall into the tube.

"'Step four,'" he read aloud, "'add contents of plastic vial... cut tip... squeeze... six... shake vigorously for ten seconds.'"

He replaced the test tube in its plastic support above the reflecting mirror. He set the stand on the most solid surface, his desk.

"Kris, we have to wait for two hours." He walked into the bedroom. "Did you hear me? We have to wait two hours now for the result. Do you want to sleep?"

"Yes," she mumbled.

"I'm going to get the paper. Do you want a bagel or anything?"

"No," she moaned, "what time is it?"

"Seven."

"Michael, it's Sunday morning."

"All right, but this is the ninth day. Don't you want to know?"

"Did you hear what I said?"

"About what?"

"Blackwell."

"I heard."

"Good."

"I'm going to get *The Times*."

"Great."

As soon as the lock clicked and Krista heard the outside door bolt she got dressed. She wore a pair of blue jeans with Michael's silk shirt. She turned the collar up and loosely brushed her hair away from her face. She stretched, as any dancer will in the morning. As she touched the flat of her palms to the floor and her head to her knees, she still hoped the result would be negative. She went up on her toes and fell forward. Then, in a straddle position, she pressed her chest to the floor. *Weren't there any other options?*

Krista went to the test tube. She sat like a cat on the arm of the chair with her chin resting on her hand, her elbow propped on her knee. She turned and peered through the Venetian blinds. The street looked stark black and white under the September sun. It looked like an old New York City postcard. She watched Michael approach from around the street corner, carrying his bagels and *The Times*. As he disappeared from view, just under the windowsill, Krista snapped open the blinds. It was as if for the first time she flipped on the light on the street where she had lived all her life.

"Kris," Michael shouted, tossing the bagels onto the kitchen counter, "the instructions say keep it out of direct sunlight."

"I just opened them."

"Have you read it?"

"No."

"Let's see." He looked into the mirror.

"Leave it alone," she said firmly.

"Okay." He picked up the newspaper.

~

An hour later he looked at the instruction leaflet again: "POSITIVE: A DARK DONUT-SHAPED BROWNISH RING (MUST HAVE A HOLE IN THE CENTER). This ring can vary in thickness and color. A ring indicates that your urine does contain pregnancy hormone, and you can assume you are pregnant. You should now consult your physician, who is best able to advise you. NEGATIVE: NO RING. JUST A DEPOSIT – NO RING."

Krista stood up. She walked towards Michael, leaned over his shoulder and looked into the mirror where the results were visible. Unimpressed, she wondered what you said when what you had always known was proven to be true. She walked back to the window. Michael thought her hips looked exceedingly narrow. Perhaps it was just the overlarge shirt. She crossed her arms over her already swollen breasts.

"Doesn't it make you feel good?" he asked. "Just a little bit?"

She turned and stared at him in horror. She went back to the desk, viewed the tube and the perfectly formed circle; looked at him without saying a word.

"Kris," he said, "I know you've made up your mind. But can't you imagine, just for a split second, us married with a baby? This time next year, playing with a little one on the beach."

"No," she answered, "I can't."

Krista dropped her head, shrouding the tube and the mirror with her long tumble of hair. She took a deep breath, and tossed the hair back over one shoulder. With perfect intent, she lifted the tube from its support and rocked it slowly. Then she shook it vigorously until everything in the circle – the entire mirror – went black.

3

Dr. Blackwell scheduled the abortion for early Wednesday. Krista had been examined late in the afternoon after the other pregnant women, those carrying their babies to full term, had come for their examinations. As they left the office one by one, glowing, Krista felt left behind, like a bad pupil kept after school. The other patients did not bother her as much as the prints hanging on the walls of the waiting room – Madonna with Sleeping Child, Madonna Enthroned with Child, Angel with Mother and Child. Some of the paintings were religious, some were not, but Krista felt unholy in a holy place. The magazines bothered her as well – *Parents, A Child's World, Good Housekeeping*. She felt as if she had got off a train at the wrong stop. Dr. Blackwell hummed a yes as soon as he began her pelvic exam, feeling the four-week growth in her womb. Krista wondered if going to a private doctor for an abortion had been the right choice. Maybe she should have gone to a clinic where no one was carrying her pregnancy to full term. The conversation in the waiting room would have been a lot easier.

After the examination, the scheduling and speaking to the nurse, Krista waited for Michael. He arrived on schedule at six. Together they sat in Dr. Blackwell's office as he traced the plastic sides of a model uterus with one immaculately manicured hand. He explained the procedure. Krista crossed her legs. In the palm of her hand she wadded and flattened a dry tissue. She asked questions: Would this endanger her chances for future pregnancies? How long would it take? Would it hurt? Would a nurse be with her the whole time?

To each question, Dr. Blackwell smiled, said *no* or *yes* and nodded reassuringly. Behind him, sixteen plastic uteruses displaying doll-like fetuses in different stages of development lined the windowsill. His own healthy, tow-haired children – three of them – were displayed in a framed photograph, sitting on a stone wall with their arms clasped snugly around each other. Krista took Michael's hand. *I wish with all my heart I knew you better. I wish I knew myself better. I wish I knew if this was the right time for us to have this child*, she thought.

Michael nervously pulled out the cuffs of his shirt from under his jacket sleeves. He spoke with Dr. Blackwell, and Krista, who had asked all of her questions, except for the one that had no answer, did not listen. Instead she studied the side of Michael's face. He said, "Yes, sir," and "No, sir," and no one said they were sorry. Only everyone could feel it.

"Such a nice couple," the old receptionist said smiling, as Krista and Michael finally stood together in the doorway of the office. A nurse in a white blouse and navy trousers introduced herself to them as Ruth. She said she would be with Krista throughout the procedure.

Krista should not eat for twenty-four hours before the surgery, which meant from Tuesday morning at ten forty-five.

"Only drink water," the receptionist warned, a look of disapproval on her face now as she handed Krista two sets of papers to sign.

"Okay," Krista said as she glanced over the document and signed twice.

She knew she must take sole responsibility for her actions. She started to cry then, and Ruth handed her a box of Kleenex. Michael held himself erect. He shook Dr. Blackwell's hand. The receptionist stomped out of the room, and Krista looked up from the papers.

"I'm sorry," she said, "I don't know why I'm crying."

"I do," Michael said.

They argued until the wee hours of Tuesday morning, Michael finally agreeing to do whatever was necessary. He said he would do what Krista wanted.

After he left for work, she mentally reviewed the previous day. She ran through her options one last time. Should she have this child after all? It was possible. At noon, Michael called to ask how she was doing. He suggested she go to a movie, to distract herself, and he also asked if he could go along with her on Wednesday.

"No," she told him firmly. "It is a very simple surgical procedure. Don't blow things out of proportion."

Tuesday night Michael ate dinner and Krista drank glass after glass of Perrier. Michael told her he was glad she could take care of things on her own because something important had come up at work. He had orchestrated a major deal for General Energy, which included several Japanese partners.

"Even your grandfather was impressed. He wants to come to the signing luncheon."

"When?" Krista asked perfunctorily.

"Tomorrow at eleven. Signing first, then lunch."

"That's great. Tomorrow night we'll celebrate."

They both stayed awake all night. Michael went over Krista's bus route to Dr. Blackwell's office three times, even sketching it for her on an index card. In the end he scrapped the whole idea. Said he thought she should take a taxi. She agreed, and they laughed uneasily. What were they getting so carried away about anyway?

While Michael showered on Wednesday morning, Krista left his apartment, went up to her own and locked the door. He called to her from the shower.

"Hey, where are you?"

When there was no answer, he waited for one minute. He called out again, and then panicked. He thought Krista had not woken. What if she died in her sleep? He laughed at his own paranoia, his stupidity, his anxiety about work and the abortion. He wrapped a towel around his waist and ran upstairs. Where was she?

"I changed my mind." He pounded on the locked apartment door. "I changed my mind. I want to take you."

"Don't be ridiculous," Krista answered through the locked door.

"Unlock this door. What are you doing in there anyway?"

"Nothing. I'm getting dressed. I want to be alone, okay?"

"No, it's not okay. You're making me anxious."

"About what?"

"You."

Krista opened the door. "Why are you making such a big thing out of nothing, something which for all practical purposes does not exist?"

"Because I love you."

She closed the door in his face.

"I want to go with you today," he insisted from the other side.

"No."

"Unlock this door!"

"It's unlocked," she answered, deliberately trying to make him feel foolish.

Michael walked into the kitchen where she was sitting at the table.

"Kris, I think I should be with you."

"Michael, let's not do this again. This is really very simple. Like taking off a wart, removing a stitch, whatever. Remember, today's your big day. Your signing luncheon."

"It can be cancelled. This is an emergency."

"It is not. Now tell me who's going to be there."

"Suzuki from Matsumoto – Abington – Krista, you're more important!"

"Michael, get out of here."

"I don't know what to do…"

"Do whatever you normally do on a Wednesday. Go to work."

"This doesn't feel like a normal Wednesday."

"Well, it is," Krista said as she pushed him out the door and closed it.

"Kris," he pounded on it once more, "call me if you change your mind."

I won't, she thought as she walked down the hall to get dressed.

What do I wear for an abortion? She sorted through the clothes in her closet while she ran the water for her bath. She momentarily watched the water from the faucet cascade and turn a delicate blue. The bath oil created tiny pellets of color. As she slipped into the hot water up to her chin, she touched her abdomen. *I am pregnant.*

She closed her eyes. She seemed to hear Helen's voice. "Ignorance is an awesome thing… the province of the simple-minded… the rich will always find what they want, what they can afford. It will be the poor who will be left to their own devices: rubber tubes, lye, Pine Sol." It was a voice she could not drown out. For a minute, Krista considered calling her mother, telling her about the abortion, about what she was preparing to do, but she slipped back under the water. This she would do on her own. Again, her mother's strident voice came to her, reading passages from her second book, *A Woman's Right to Life*.

It is a frightening thing, controlling one's own fate. What does it mean when we have a hand in our own destiny? That we should have more respect for life than to consider it a twist of fate, that we should plan for it, not allowing it to be viewed as some mystical work of predestination in which we have no choice. Can women bear responsibility for the decision-making process without bearing guilt? I bore a child against my will, and do not think I have not suffered anger, oppression.

No doubt, Krista thought, everything my mother says is true, but what do I tell this Little One? What do I tell this being which, from its conception, I have felt? What do I say to this other life that is not mine? I can distinguish its separateness. Reflecting on the moment of conception, that instant flooding of light, Krista wondered what other women might feel. Was it similar to her own experience? Surely not, she thought, because, if it were, she would have heard about it. She would have read about it. Helen would have mentioned it… but no one had. Krista blamed her body, her dancer's body, which had been trained to react to the slightest stimulus. She chastised herself for being too sensitive, and dusted her body with talc. She tossed the towel over the sink.

In the living room, she sat cross-legged in the overstuffed armchair. It was too early yet for the trip to the East Side. She heard Michael close the front door, and she cried, wrapping her arms around herself. She heard him whistle. In her mind's eye, she saw him walk to 7th Avenue, hail a taxi, and for a split second she was sorry he was not coming with her. She thought about prayer, and did the only thing she knew to do.

"Little One," she said, "please wait for me. Little Spirit, there will be a time when it is right, I promise. I will know then, just as now I do not. Little One, please wait. I am sorry, I am terribly sorry."

Krista cried, making amends for what she thought might just be the wrong choice. *How can anything feel so right and so wrong in the same instant?*

"Little Spirit," she cried out loud, "I do not want to let you go. Little One, please wait."

Krista repeated the words several times, to herself and out loud. They were the same words she'd once heard on the Island at the close of season late one night on the narrow walkway to the lighthouse. She had gone to the spot alone to watch the night sky and to listen to the surf wearily rolling itself to extinction on the sand. She had gone to see if somewhere between Jupiter and Orion she might catch that glimpse of her father for which she always hoped. Krista knew it was whimsical of her but she liked thinking about him this way.

She knew it was Deirdre coming down the walk as soon as the first steps resounded against the wooden boards. Krista wanted to rise and run, but there was no time. Instead she had moved into the shadows. Her friend sat with her feet dangling over the water at the end of the walk. Deirdre's shoulders rose and fell. Dry grasses whistled, and buoys tinkled in the harbor. Deirdre spoke to herself. A bicycle bell rang twice far away. Krista could hear what her friend was saying.

"I couldn't. I couldn't have another."

Silence washed over the beach. Krista held her knees against her chest. She smelled brine, rotting seaweed and a beach fire. A skip darted between the anchored boats, its light searching the face of the water. Krista felt the sand in her tennis shoes.

"Wait," Deirdre said, "wait, Little Spirit. There will come a time."

Deirdre jumped instantly to her feet and ran the full length of the walk back to the street. The words seemed to hang in the air behind her. *Wait, Little Spirit. There will come a time.* Krista never mentioned that evening to anyone, especially not to Deirdre, because she had not quite understood, and because she respected those she thought might also be searching, like her, for the dead.

Sitting in the overstuffed armchair, waiting to make the trip to the East Side, it came to Krista what Deirdre had been talking about and to whom she had been speaking. As they had that night, her words seemed to hang in mid-air. Krista repeated them. She said the same short prayer to the child she had chosen not to birth.

～

Krista hid behind the large-framed sunglasses she borrowed from her mother's dresser. On a cross-town bus a passenger said hello. Krista nodded back. *I'm on my way to an abortion. How 'bout you? Sunny day, isn't it?* The passenger returned to reading her paper. Krista imagined jumping to her feet and telling the whole bus: *I'm going to abort a fetus. How does that grab you?* She saw herself interviewing each passenger. She would ask their opinion, and as if pulling petals from a daisy – *he loves me, he loves me not* – she would decide. Abortion yes, abortion no. She

47

would let this random sample of human beings be her judge and jury. That, she thought, would be much simpler than having to decide for herself.

She crossed her legs and tapped her foot. She looked like a hundred other young women in New York who might be dancers, lawyers, teachers, thieves, or perhaps on their way to see their obstetrician for a safe abortion. Suddenly, Krista wanted only one thing. She wanted it all over with so that things could return to normal. She would be as she had been. She would even go back to studying dance with Madame Chevalier.

The office she had last seen late in the afternoon looked different at nine thirty in the morning. A baby murmured, a woman at full term breathed heavily, and another with her pregnancy barely showing flipped through a magazine. The paintings seemed to loom even larger. A toddler pushed a gaily colored train over the carpet. Krista wanted to run but Ruth intercepted her.

"Mrs. Bourne."

"Miss, Ms., I'm not married," Krista corrected her.

The nurse remained unfazed by this.

"Your husband asked that you call him."

"Michael?"

Krista took the piece of paper on which a number had been noted and dialed from the receptionist's desk.

"Krista," Michael answered immediately, "thank God! I didn't think you were going to call. Listen, this may sound stupid, really stupid… but I want to marry you. I do! We can have this baby. It's all right really, to do it this way. I love you. We don't have to be married first. You don't have to have this abortion. I want the baby."

"Don't be stupid."

Krista hung up the phone as Dr. Blackwell walked a patient in her eighth month from one examining room to the next. Just when Krista thought she did not know what to do, Ruth appeared from a back office and ushered her outside.

"Dr. Blackwell uses facilities across the street for abortions," she explained.

The traffic at ten o'clock was congested. The nurse held Krista's elbow and they both darted through the oncoming cars.

In a smoke-filled waiting room, men waited for their wives or girlfriends. They lounged, stood in corners, held various reading material on their laps and drank Coca-Cola. For the first time Krista felt afraid. She allowed the nurse to guide her. She signed another set of papers.

"Sit here and when Dr. Blackwell arrives," she was told, "you will take your clothes off over there. I will give you a paper bag for your things."

Krista was astonished. The nurse was actually smoking a cigarette, sliding the pack from the front pocket of her white uniform. She even asked Krista if she wanted one.

After considering it, she politely said, "No, thank you." *I just want to know if it hurts.* Her gut felt hard and solid as a rock. She looked at each passing woman. None of them met her eyes. She heard the hushed whispers of counseling as one woman explained something to another, using a similar model to the uterus Dr. Blackwell displayed in his office. One woman spoke and the other woman listened, except for an impatient "Yes, yes, yes." Krista counted ponytails. They all wore ponytails; even her own hair had been pulled back in a tight band, though she couldn't remember doing it herself. She fidgeted with the loose ends pulled over her shoulder.

It was ten forty-five. Krista asked Ruth about Dr. Blackwell. She started to ask about the procedure but the nurse stopped her.

"I'll be right back."

Krista studied the women around her, the ones without private doctors. This place resembled a factory. Women in, women out. Just when Krista thought fear would overtake her and that she would leave – maybe Michael had been right – Dr. Blackwell arrived.

"Hello, Ms. Bourne," he said, "sorry to keep you waiting. Please get undressed."

Ruth reappeared. She handed Krista a brown paper bag.

"Put your things in here."

Krista headed for a small dressing stall. She pulled off her sweater, her skirt, her socks and panties. Placing her hand on her belly she whispered a little prayer. *Very soon, it will be all over.* She wondered for the briefest of moments whose life it was she was taking. Her own? She willed herself not to cry. What would these other women think? Did it affect them at all? Did they also kiss the tips of their fingers and touch them lightly to their belly? Did they tell their Little Ones to wait? *Idiot. What am I thinking? What would they think if they knew I was afraid? No, not just afraid, but scared out of my wits. This feels like a sin.*

The nurse tapped on the dressing-room door. Krista

took her belongings with her into a green-tiled room. Two other nurses told her to use the small bathroom, to try and urinate. They took her clothes and positioned her on a steel-topped table. No one smiled. No one said hello or good morning. It was all business. No one said anything that was not strictly necessary. Krista watched a nurse fill a syringe, and recalled she detested needles. She tried to catch someone's eye. She did not see Ruth. *Wasn't this the procedure? Wasn't she supposed to be around?* Krista wanted the comfort of someone's hand. *Michael.* Where was he? Lunch, she recalled, and wished him luck. Dr. Blackwell darted in and out. She wanted to tell him she did not want to be knocked out. The two nurses strapped her legs into the stirrups. A green oxygen tank was rolled forward.

"Doctor," Krista said.

He looked her in the eye and, with a professional nod, said, "I'll be right back."

Krista took in the white ceiling. Her legs were tied down with black bands. They were strapped twice.

"Count from one hundred backwards," someone said.

Krista focused on the ceiling. The last thing she remembered was the pale palm of the black nurse who took her hand and then the tears when she started to cry.

~

"Shock!" Krista heard the call like the cry of a gull, shrieking far off yet directly over her head.

"Pressure falling—"

51

She felt herself tumbling, turning, the speed of her descent startling. Her body asserted itself long before her mind. She sensed a tight knot, as if every ounce of her being had been drawn up and nailed to the center of her spine, only to be gutted. Muscle and bone ached. It was as if she had done battle and lost. She began to hear other things: voices, metal, pages being shuffled.

"Oxygen!" someone shouted.

"Miss Bourne," another person asked, "where does it hurt?"

Krista lay still in the fetal position, continuing to fall as if everything that bound her to life had been cut away. *Who were these people?* She opened her eyes. The light was excruciating, and she could not see their faces clearly. She felt nauseous and reached for her abdomen. She could only feel a complete and utter sense of loss, one for which she had been unprepared. For four weeks she had experienced the life expanding within her. Now she felt only death.

"Adrenalin!" a male voice called out.

"Miss Bourne," a vaguely familiar voice asked, "where does it hurt?"

Krista turned her head, saw the doctor's dark hair, the white uniform coat and the sweater beneath. She could not distinguish the face. She touched her belly again. Nothing else existed. Then she felt her pulse, wrapped in the black Velcro grip of an orderly taking her blood pressure. She turned her head again, struggling to regain consciousness. Faces appeared as if through gauze. In that instant, she knew what it was she would do. She would never go back.

Her body took over. *I'm not coming out. I'm not coming out.* Krista lost consciousness.

"Emergency!"

A scuffle ensued. Her knees were forced away from her chest, her arms from over her heart. She cried and felt ready to attack. She would claw, bite. She felt the place where her body had reared up against the instruments and she recalled now why she ached. The nurse motioned everyone away. The gesture triggered a wave over Krista's closed eyes. Her lids stirred heavily. She could see but it seemed a veil had been placed over the scene. *Who was this woman?* Her face was warm, eyes kind, but Krista ran the tip of her tongue over each incisor anyway. She was as prepared as any cornered wounded animal might be to fight with whatever strength she had left. *Where was the fetus?*

"Miss Bourne, tell me where it hurts."

"Everywhere," Krista answered.

"Show me."

There was another flutter of activity. Someone whispered.

"Miss Bourne," the woman said, "do you know a Michael Parks?"

The gauze before her eyes faded away. Krista could see again. She took a deep breath.

"That's it," the woman said, "nice and easy."

Krista forced her legs down, felt the sanitary pad belted to her body, and willed herself to sit up. *Michael.*

"Miss Bourne, Mr. Parks is waiting for you."

She lay still, making an inventory of her body. Hands,

feet, toes. *What was missing? What remained?* First thing, she thought, I must get up. I have a plan.

"Mr. Parks," the woman said, more insistently, "is in the waiting room."

Krista sat up. The nurse and the medics left.

"We thought you'd never stop crying," the woman in the opposite cot said as Krista pulled her clothing from the paper bag and started to dress.

"What?"

"You've been crying for ages. Since they brought you in."

"I don't remember," she said listlessly.

"You were. It scared them. Me too. Think you were doing it for all of us."

"I did cry a little," Krista said, "just before I went under. I think I recall, before – no after – the injection."

"You didn't have a local?"

"No."

"You were lucky. I watched the whole thing."

"Watched it?"

Krista saw that she was standing in the center of the room, between two parallel rows of beds containing women in varying states of consciousness. Many of them were crying silently. Some were not. Krista thought through her plan. She had to get home first, get the car. But where... where would she do it?

"Take some juice," a nurse said, without looking up from the desk where she sat filling out forms.

"Yes," Krista answered, picking up the plastic cup. Another woman, still in her hospital gown, spoke on the phone. Did Krista hear her correctly? She was making a tennis date. The courts. In an hour. Krista dropped the remains of her juice into a metal waste can. She felt nauseous. *Michael.* She saw the corridor from which she had walked earlier, and just when she thought she might faint, she heard that familiar voice ring out once more.

"Miss Bourne. There you are. Mr. Parks is this way."

The woman ushered Krista to an exit and into the waiting room through which she had first entered the clinic.

"Thank you," Krista said as she now recalled this woman.

"For what?"

"For holding my hand," she said, "before I went under."

The nurse touched her shoulder sympathetically and then went through the swinging door back to the clinic, leaving a brief stirring in the air behind her. *Michael.* Krista saw him then. He smiled. She saw the three-piece suit, the briefcase and the gold watch. How far, she thought, he had come since that first day in Central Park in his cycling shorts and T-shirt. She recalled that promise of a first telephone call. He had not failed her then, and he did not fail her now.

"I had to come," he said.

"I know."

"Don't be angry with me."

"I'm not."

"Let's go home."

To die, Krista thought as Michael hailed a yellow cab.

4

Dr. Blackwell's office remained full of smiling pregnant women. It was the last place Krista wanted to be.

"Michael," she begged, "let's just go home."

"Kris," he pointed out, "the nurse said Dr. Blackwell wants to see you. No excuses. You almost went into shock. Do you realize that? The seriousness of it? He needs to see you. I want him to see you. Hang in there. It won't take long."

"Room four. Dr. Blackwell will be with you soon," the receptionist told them. It seemed she knew what had happened and hadn't the heart to wear her disapproving expression. Krista acquiesced, leaning heavily on Michael and letting him lead her.

Dr. Blackwell's examination was quick, routine, gentle. In fifteen minutes he had not only checked Krista but also fitted her with a new diaphragm.

"Hold this up to the light occasionally," he said, "to check for cracks."

So that's how life gets in, Krista thought. *Through the cracks.*

"You look fully recovered," he enthused, as if congratulating her for something. "Let me see you on Monday. Just pop in and, of course, refrain from intercourse for the next six weeks. Lose the weight you've gained, especially if you are going to keep dancing. You are a dancer, correct? I know you have not gained much, but you will feel better if you do. If you bleed at all, even a small amount, call me straight away."

In the taxi Krista felt faint. The color drained from her face as she rested it against Michael's shoulder.

"Why didn't you tell Dr. Blackwell?" Michael demanded.

"Tell him what?" Krista asked.

"That you don't feel well."

"I'm okay. I just want to go home."

"Kris, where does it hurt?" he insisted, his forehead creased with worry.

"I can't talk right now. I'm too hot. Too tired." She rolled away from him and tilted her head back against the seat. "I need to vomit," she said, "only there's nothing left to vomit."

Krista managed a laugh then, as if to say, "Michael, relax, I'm okay." Her face felt as if it might crack.

"Do you want to stop?" he asked.

"For what?"

"Something to eat."

"No," she answered, rolling back towards him, pulling her knees up a little. "I really just want to go home, and to sleep. I feel groggy. Out of it."

He took her arm and looped it through his. "Everything will be fine."

Krista closed her eyes. She knew all the stops and starts, the rights and lefts, that preceded the townhouse on

Bank Street. Michael opened the door to the cab, holding it with his elbow and briefcase while supporting Krista with his other arm. She felt weak, drained.

"You should eat," he said. "That's all I want to say."

"No," she said again as she undressed, dropping her clothes where she stood and crawling between the cool sheets. Michael set two mugs and the teapot on a tray.

"Are you sure?" He couldn't think of anything else to do for her.

"Do you know what I really feel like?"

"Corned beef on rye?"

"Oh, God."

"No?"

"I feel as if I've been deboned or submerged or – I can't explain it – I feel I can't feel." And with that, she passed into the deep sleep she craved.

Michael turned off the water he was boiling for tea. From the living room he thought he heard her whimper. It sounded like a child's cry, muffled and far away. He walked to the bedroom and stood in the doorway, removed his already loosened tie and lay down beside her.

Krista first descended deep into sleep, then felt herself rouse into a sort of semi-wakefulness. She awoke abruptly, fighting hard to recall where she was and with whom. More sleep. Stirring again, she saw Michael and remembered everything. *Would the memory of this day ever fade?* She worked her way back into a numb sort of slumber. She didn't want to see, hear, feel. Then the images came – a loose scalpel, a wheel from a pram, a child's face. They flew at her, coming from seemingly nowhere. *What have I done?* She felt she couldn't breathe. Her heart beat painfully fast. It hurt. This was different from any exertion she'd experienced as a dancer. She was terrified. The anesthetic could no longer deaden the images – the blood, the spittle and the soft baby toes – that came whirling at her through her desperate sleep.

She began to awaken. She felt herself to be in the center of a whirlwind. As she rose through each spiral, she saw a face, a figure, a scene she did not want to recall. The turning she experienced was the slow, weighted twisting of a cockpit. She perspired. Her own weight increased. The sun was blinding. The air hot, thin. And somewhere below, Daddy was telling her to spot Ilsa's apple tree. If she could just see the house, that apple tree, the white blossoms, the yellow center... She struggled.

Krista could no longer determine if she was awake or asleep. *Have I gone mad?* Her breathing came in hard, fast intakes that seemed beyond her control. Her eyes darted around the room. She felt surrounded by something opaque, wet, hard and glistening. She did not recognize the room. *Was this the inside of the shell? Was this the shell I promised to save for Daddy, the one he never came to collect?* She ran her palms blindly over its surface, searching for a way out. When she finally saw it – a thin filament of gold – it immediately disappeared.

Krista sat bolt upright. Michael lay beside her, lost in sleep. Something came to mind, and she fought hard to recall where she recognized it from:

... like a Hoover... same idea... vacuums the walls of the uterus... drawing it up, through and out the tube.

Start to finish? Six minutes. May feel a stitch, a slight cramp, nothing different than a bit of premenstrual discomfort. Perhaps some spotting… But all in all, painless.

Painless. Painless? Krista kept her knees to her chest, cradled in her arms. *Painless?* I feel pain, I feel gutted, she thought. And the pain in her gut was equaled only by the pain in her heart. She held still, as if keeping a tenuous balance, as if the slightest motion would send her toppling in any number of directions. She searched for the ceiling, the thing she once called *the inside*, the cool galaxy of sapphire blue. There was nothing, only a memory, a peeling ceiling half filled with cardboard stars. And in place of the comfort it had once brought her, now there was nothing but emptiness.

She would rather die, she decided, than continue to feel this. She didn't want to know this pain. She didn't want the memory of this pain, and she feared it would be with her forever. *How can I live?* she asked herself. She watched Michael. He rose, opened the blinds and let in the late afternoon sun. In blue jeans and a polo shirt, with his hair freshly brushed, he looked as if nothing had happened, as if nothing had changed. She listened to the sounds from the bathroom, imagined him throwing water over his face, then cupping a mouthful to gargle. His summer flip-flops slapped the hardwood floor.

… six minutes… all in all, painless.

"Sleeping Beauty," he called out, "tea?"

She held still. *Tea? I want to die.* But not here, she decided, not in Michael's bed, beneath Helen's apartment, in D.B.'s house. *But I do want to die.* I could, she thought, die now, from complications. Bleed to death. She refused to answer Michael and feigned sleep. *I have the right to die.* Decisions, she thought, my own decisions. She turned, pulling one pillow towards her chest and the other under her head.

"Are you awake? What do you want?" he asked anxiously, bending over her.

"Nothing. I don't want anything."

"Krista, you have to eat. It's been over twenty-four hours, you've suffered a significant amount of stress."

"I don't want to eat, okay?"

"I made tea. Jasmine with honey."

"Stop it, Michael."

"Stop what?"

"Stop babying me."

"Do you want tea or don't you?"

"I want to sleep."

"So sleep."

Again, Krista closed her eyes. Waiting, she felt Michael enter and exit like a phantom, touching her forehead lightly, sitting silently on the edge of the bed. A gaping darkness, a hunger for which she could not find the words, began to loom all about her. The very room seemed dangerous, as if she could step off it into infinity. She felt the extreme turn of events, the catapult from fullness to nothing. She felt as if all the blood had been flushed from her veins.

"Okay," Michael said in a singsong voice. He pulled the blanket over her chest, rousing her in the same instant, "it's time for you to rejoin the living. You have ten seconds to say, 'Yes, dear, I'd love a cup of tea,' or, without any hesitation, I will begin the force feed."

"Okay, okay," she mumbled into the pillow.

"Good, that's what I need to hear."

He kissed her gently, leaning his forehead close, and took her slender shoulders in his hands. The minute his flesh touched hers the pain was unbearable. She understood why she could not forget. *It was Michael's fault. His presence.* How could things possibly return to normal with him hovering over her like this? It was his fault she saw her ceiling as flaking and tawdry. He had come too close. He had violated her inside space. He was the invader. None of this would have happened if it had not been for him. And none of it would go away until he went away.

In an instant, Krista saw what she must do. After all, this apartment, this house, belonged to Daddy Bourne, to *her* family. She could make Michael go away, just as easily as she could rid herself of an unwanted pregnancy. She took the teacup he offered from the blue tray. He stirred in the honey. Krista blew tiny ripples across the surface of the red tea. Michael's face appeared to her as if from behind a thin veil. It was the way the nurses' faces had looked when she came out from under the anesthetic. *Cut him out, remove him.* She watched his lips move. *What was he saying?*

The hot tea hit her stomach. Krista relaxed. Everything, she suddenly realized, would be fine, would and could return to normal. All of this, she thought, will be as if it never happened. She sat up, straightened her spine. She felt almost regal. *Don't frighten him.* She slowly sipped her tea, holding the cup close to her lips, as if that very gesture would hide all of her thoughts from her lover. *What was he saying?* She couldn't hear a thing. *He must not catch me. Everything must go smoothly.* She returned the half-empty cup to the tray, pulled her knees to her chest, and brought the blanket up and under her chin. She continued to eye Michael, like a threatened animal waiting to seize its moment to escape.

"How do you feel?" he asked impatiently.

"Fine. Much better, but still a bit shaky." Pure evasion tactics. *He must know the truth. He must be made to confront the awful, empty, bleeding thing I have become.* But not right now. She planned carefully. She could make him, the abortion, the pain, disappear. *I must get upstairs, away from him.*

"Do you want to eat?"

"No, the tea was perfect. Hit the spot." *There is nothing I want from you, ever again. Except to be out of my sight. There was nothing I ever really wanted from you. You were merely pretty, comfortable and convenient. My hunger is too great. It is a need you will never be able to fill.* "No," she said, "I'm not terribly hungry."

She dressed. Her knees felt weak, her body unnaturally cold. She wore Michael's shirt and her own blue jeans. She recalled the brown paper bag, the clinic, her clothes.

"Stay in bed," Michael suggested.

"No, I'm going upstairs, need to feed Cosmos."

"You're not going upstairs! You're better off here. Now, what do you want to eat? I'll fix something."

"Michael, for the last time, I don't want anything to eat. Maybe you eat when you're hurt but I don't, okay? I'm the animal that likes to hide in the corner, curl up, lick my wounds…"

"Calm down, cut the dramatics. I've had…"

"No, Michael, it's just beginning. I've had enough. This, all of this, is *your fault.* And I want you out of here."

"Out of where?"

"Here, my grandfather's house."

"Krista, lie down…"

"Did you hear me? It's over between you and me, and I want you out of this house immediately. I don't ever want to see you again. Do you understand? None of this would have happened if I hadn't brought you here, none of it." She leaned heavily on the dining-room table, recalled the miniature lab, the test kit, the black ring, the mirror she had shaken until it went blank.

Michael recognized her distress. "Tell me," he said, "tell me one reason why now, after it's all over? This is all wrong. See how you feel tomorrow. We can discuss it then."

"No, I know what I want. I want you out of here now, this minute. There are no reasons, I simply want you out of my life. It's not difficult to understand – it's over. Did you think it would last forever? Did you seriously entertain notions of marriage?"

"Krista, you're acting like a lunatic."

"I have that right, too, you know."

"Get back in bed."

"I'm going to my own bed."

"You can't."

"I can't?"

"Krista, no one else is home."

"You're not my mother, why should you care? You're no one to me now. So leave me, get out."

"Kris…"

He looked like a stranger, she realized. Or, no, someone she vaguely recognized. A handsome man she once saw take third in a race in Central Park.

"Michael, get out of here," she told him, carefully keeping her voice low and conversational. "I hate you, do you understand? I hate you."

His forehead creased in incomprehension. He couldn't be hearing this.

"But… I asked you to marry me."

"Oh, yes, how could I forget? At the last minute, you assuaged your guilt. Or was it your responsibility? You didn't go in there with me. I went in on my own – *on my own*. You know it, and I know it. Now, I want you out. This second. There is no forever."

"Who's talking about forever? Just calm down. Tomorrow morning…"

Her assumed patience snapped.

"Get out, damn you!"

"Don't damn me, damn your…" Michael stopped talking. He didn't want to lose control. He had made himself a promise – to see Krista through this. "I don't know what else to say to you. Except that I love you."

"Say it then," she taunted him. "Damn yourself."

"Krista, I'm trying to be patient here. I've suffered too."

"No, you haven't. You haven't begun to suffer, and there's nothing you can feel that would compare to this. Nothing."

"Come here." He made an attempt to embrace her.

"Don't!" she screamed. "Don't touch me."

"Okay, okay," he said, backing off, his eyes wide with alarm. "Let's talk about this rationally. You hurt, but the abortion…"

"The abortion," she said, mocking him.

"An abortion…"

"Okay, Michael, tell me about it."

"You were vacuumed out."

"Explain it to me, Michael."

"Describe it?"

"Yes."

"I… I can't. I can't." He could not picture what she had been through.

"Well, let me tell you then. Dr. Blackwell performs a combination vacuum and D&C. D&C, Michael, dilation and curettage. The cervix – you know where that is, don't you?"

"Don't be facetious."

"My cervix was dilated by passing a series of metal dilators, each a little bigger than the last, into the opening. Then my womb was scraped clean by a surgical scoop. Then hoovered. Do you understand? You may think a fetus is nothing more than a spoonful of cells. Okay, think that, but the pain is extraordinary. There is pain."

"Whoever said there wasn't? Come on, Kris… what do you want? A medal?"

"No, I want you out of here, now."

"Do you want to talk with a counselor?"

"No, I just want you out."

"I'm not leaving."

"Oh, yes, you are. It's only a question of whether you do it now or wait until D.B. tells you to go, which will be a matter of hours." Up the street a truck stopped, brakes squealing. Michael and Krista fell silent. More city sounds crept into the apartment.

"Okay, Krista. It won't take me any time to get out of here, forget the whole thing. But for you, it's going to take years, maybe a lifetime. You brought this abortion on yourself. You wanted it. You wanted it like some kind of merit badge. You wanted it the way some men want Mount Everest. Or maybe to impress your mother."

"Or a million-dollar deal?"

He recoiled slightly, still guilty that he had gone into the office instead of staying with her.

"Or a million-dollar deal. This, Krista, was part of your initiation, another step in your spaced-out idea of becoming a woman. Well, let me tell you something: it's not working. You might be nineteen, but you act like a spoiled seven-year-old, still waiting for her daddy to come home. But at least Helen will be proud of you now. Her daughter wasn't a victim of circumstance. Her daughter went blithely out and took a life – killed – to assert her own independence. Only now that she has to face the music, she can't handle it."

"Don't talk to me about killing, because if I killed—"

"There is no 'if'. How does it feel? Or can you not feel the difference between life and death? Between full and empty? You're only half here ninety-nine percent of the time, holding yourself back like you're some kind of prize. You better wake up to yourself, lady!"

"Stop it. I want you quickly and quietly out of this apartment, this house, my—"

"Your life," he finished for her. "Easier said than aborted." He tossed clothes wildly, randomly, from drawers and closets, into a leather valise. "You know, I did want to marry you once, when you were innocent. I suppose I did think this," he motioned to the walls, the ceiling, "you, General Energy, all of it had a forever feeling. Not magic, just safe. Comfortable. That's how I picture love – pictured love – safe, comfortable."

"Well, you were wrong," she told him, though she had to force the words out.

"Oh, yeah," he said, "I was wrong." He closed and locked the suitcase. "Or maybe I was wrong about loving you. But anyone can make a mistake. I am leaving, and not because you are throwing me out. I'm leaving because you, Krista, with your endless self-concern, are like bad stock, going down. So I'm selling up... bailing out."

"Fine," she told him. She turned to the door and slipped back the top bolt. The second bolt jammed. She tugged, slammed the knob with the heel of her palm. She felt terrified, as if now she would never escape, never be free from him. "Open this!" she screamed.

"Open it yourself," he answered. "You let yourself in, you let yourself out."

Again, she desperately hammered the knob, tried the bolt. Then she stood still and quiet, as if submitting to the door being locked, as if she were prepared to accept the worst and remain there forever.

From behind Michael watched her breathing, the rise and fall of her thin shoulder blades through his shirt. He'd been kidding himself. He still loved her.

He took her by the shoulders, and she leaned submissively into his chest, thinking, *Will nothing make him go away?* If she told him she did not want the child only because it was *his* child, would he go away then? Would he leave if he was told it wasn't the child she didn't want, it was him? She thought of several lies she could tell. But somehow, as Michael held her in his arms, she knew he would never leave. He was steadfast, loyal, and she would stay there, locked in his arms forever, kept from the past forever. He would never let her retreat, disappear into her once-safe inside.

"Please," she whispered, turning into his chest, "please let me out. I'm sorry. I'm terribly sorry, but I do not love you." Then she began to cry, and the huge, gaping, empty hunger she felt in her gut began to gnaw at her.

"Hey," he said, brushing his lips against her forehead, taking her hair in both his hands, lifting it over her shoulders on both sides. "Nobody said you have to love me. We're just friends. We've always been just friends. You live upstairs, and I live down."

"No," she said, "we've never even been friends. You know it, and I know it." She spoke into his chest, into his shirt pocket. "I don't even know who you are. I just brought you home because you were pretty. You were the prettiest man in the park. And then you became a part of everything, and it was as if you were always, had always, been here, like…"

"Don't say it, Kris."

"Like…"

"Don't, Kris."

"Like a…"

"Dog?"

"No, a brother."

He drew in his breath sharply.

"You know, I finally see the whole set-up. Suddenly it's all very clear to me." He unlocked the door, opening it wide for her. "I understand the whole abortion, from beginning to end."

"No, Michael."

"Yes, Kris. I know now why you took the life of my first child."

"I didn't take—"

"Call it what you want. You made the decision. You did away with what would have been my child. And I know why."

"No," she said, "you don't."

"Very simple, very clear, Krista. All of this, getting rid of the fetus, getting rid of me. I understand. It all makes sense now. It's because I'm poor."

"Yes," she said, hearing his words fall like a tumbler in a lock. "Yes." And she agreed to the only thing he would accept. "I had an abortion, and I'm asking you to leave because you are poor, come from nowhere, have no family. Think about it. You have nothing to offer me. Absolutely nothing I don't already have. You live under our roof and work for my grandfather. Why should I let you leech off me any longer?"

"I knew it," he said, brown eyes turning black and empty.

"Yes," she said, aware of the pain she was inflicting, "it is because you are poor."

5

Krista locked the door to her apartment behind her. She listened for Michael's footsteps on the stairs.

"God, please don't let him follow me," she whispered.

It had been so simple, telling him it was because he was poor, telling him that lie. In fact, he had practically told himself. She just agreed. The room spun in the twilight, the time of day she liked best, patterned by the shadows of the leaves swaying in the wind and the headlights of the traffic heading home. Krista felt confused. Everything seemed to have a different life, older, not belonging to her. The phone rang, and she let it ring. The painting above the mantle, the loft bed over the sofa, the stereo, the albums, the collection of oversized books. Nothing looked familiar. The animal skin on the floor appeared for the first time as something dead. It was no longer simply a soft rug upon which Krista might curl up in front of a fire, to read a book, to listen to music or to dream.

Everything had another dimension. One she had previously refused to recognize. Krista attempted to divert her fear. *Beginnings and ends. Yes, things die. There is a natural arc. People leave and don't come back.* On the teak sideboard there was a triptych of photographs: Charles, Helen and Krista. Father, Mother, Baby. She turned them on their faces. She picked up a tarnished brass bowl, and as if it might help her locate her identity, began to read the old campaign buttons stashed inside: Kennedy for President, Witches Heal, The Goddess Saves. No wiser, she set the bowl back on the lace doily.

In the kitchen she threw water on her face. Helen's kitchen, she thought to herself, my mother's kitchen. She noted details as she stood struggling to recall something, something she was sure was important: vitamins, herbs, cookbooks. On the counter lay Helen's paper, an assignment for a graduate-school course: "Repercussions of the Weaning: Feminists Born After *The Feminine Mystique*" by Helen Bourne. Krista picked up the short manuscript, flipping through the pages. It had been on the counter the entire time Helen toured, yet it appeared unfamiliar. The paper was about her, about her generation. Who was Helen Bourne? And why would she write a paper on the effects of The Movement? *She is my mother.* Krista looked through the long windows at the cats stretched out along the railing of the deck.

"Christmas, Cosmos, Allegro!" she called out.

A cramp knifed her belly. She doubled over, then started to cry uncontrollably. She heard doors downstairs slam. The only other human life in the brownstone was leaving. *Michael, I'm sorry, I'm terribly sorry. Forgive me, please forgive me.* Again the cramping seemed to send out malignant tentacles. Her entire circulation seemed to tighten as if intent on strangling her. Krista felt the void inside her like an empty cradle. In anger she shouted at the ceiling fan and to Michael who stood outside hailing a cab.

"You tell me where it came from, and I'll tell you where it went. Do you hear me, Michael?"

Krista beat her fists on the counter. Sliding her back down the kitchen wall, she squatted and cried. *If only I could make it all go away.* She acknowledged the physical pain. That, she could understand. But what she could not fathom was the excruciating ache in her heart. *A full extension*, she kept hearing her dance teacher say. *A full extension.* Cold and disorienting fear spread through her. Was this how it was going to be for her always? What had she done? She recalled the passage, printed on yellowing paper.

… like a Hoover… same idea… vacuums the walls of the uterus… drawing it up, through and out the tube. Start to finish? Six minutes. May feel a stitch, a slight cramp, nothing different than a bit of premenstrual discomfort. Perhaps some spotting… But all in all, painless.

I must go to the bed. I must get into bed. I need to sleep.

Krista called out to the cats again and again. This time Cosmos heard and followed her into the bedroom, which had once been the nursery. The room was dark, with the shades still drawn from the last night she slept there with Michael. *The night I conceived.* The satin comforter lay just where she left it, loosely folded at the foot of the bed. The room was chilly with a hint of autumn. Krista felt another sharp cramp and sat on the edge of the bed. She lay down and pulled the blanket up and over her shoulders. Shivering, she watched as Cosmos sat on the dresser, cleaning his fine fur, his head dipping in short regular thrusts. *As if nothing has happened.*

In the twilight the stars on the ceiling looked as they once had. They glittered, they shone. Or did they? No matter how diligently Krista forced herself, she could not see them with the child's eye she once had. Even the twilight did not help the illusion; it did not make her father's artistry shine the way it once had. The magic was gone. Or was it the hope?

Krista could not will herself to sleep. She stared dry-eyed at the ceiling. *Why hadn't her mother had it repainted? Why had it remained like this for all these years, a constant reminder?* Krista held her sides. Anger welled in her.

"So whose fault is it? Whose fault?" she cried out.

She sat up, looked around the room. Photographs of her father lined the walls. On the dresser there was one picture of Helen and a portrait of Ilsa and Daddy Bourne. By the door was the watercolor of Isadora Duncan that Ilsa had given Krista many years before when she had first studied dance. She walked over to the painting of the dancer.

"Freedom?" she said aloud, almost laughing. She tore the painting from its hook, and threw it across the room, against the wall. *Rubbish.* The glass popped out from the frame, cracking down the center. Krista knocked all the photographs from the dresser, then the wall, every image of her father. She managed to heave and drag the dresser to the center of the room.

In the hall closet, Krista rummaged through boxes, coats and stray shoes to find what she was looking for: the large grey toolbox. Opening the lid, she searched like a madwoman but couldn't find them. In the kitchen, under the sink, she finally found what she was looking for: two cans of black spray-paint.

In her own room, she mounted the dresser and shook one of the cans. She focused on where to begin. Then, without hesitation, sprayed a wide dark arc, extending her arm its full length from the socket, swinging it back and forth as far as she could reach. She divided the makeshift sky and let the black paint bleed. She painted long, looping spirals. Then she braided a long thread back through the spiral, and traced a black circle around the perimeter of the room. Jumping from the dresser to the bed, to the chair, and back again, she laughed aloud. She had almost forgotten about the pain. From the top of the bookshelves, she began spraying concentric circles, one inside the next, until she reached the center, the zenith of her father's ceiling. That spot she sprayed into a solid, dark mass.

At random, she dashed the sky with triangles, pyramids, squares. Finally, she sprayed a thickly delineated diamond. With the ceiling almost totally filled, she began sketching eyes on the space that was left, then on the walls around her. She gave them long lashes, deep lids and wide pupils. She laughed again, falling onto the bed, looking up at the place where once there had been sky. It hung dark and dense above her head, decorated with eyes like the fanning tail of a peacock. She lay there watching the memory of the sky spiral away, caught up in madness after destroying the heaven she had left on her bedroom ceiling for so long.

She grabbed the other can. Armed now with both of them, she further attacked the walls. Black lines obliterated family portraits. From the center of the bed, she brought her arms forward with the cans trailing their jet-black exhaust. She focused her attention on the mirror, on the strange face she saw there. *Is that me?* Again, she drew concentric circles, beginning with the dark wood frame, and moving further and further inward. As she reached the center, Krista could not stop, even as the paint pooled and ran down the glass. Her face was completely gone. The cans were empty. She threw one then the next at the mirror, shattering it. As she surveyed the wreckage, she saw the words again, freed from the page, floating before her:

… *all in all, painless… painless… six minutes.*

She began a mad hunt. *Where have I read these words? The lie.* Her intuition told her that they were very near. *In this apartment, I know those words are in this apartment. Somewhere.*

The lie, she asked herself, where is the lie?

She stood at the window for a few minutes. An elderly woman from across the street stared back. They made eye contact. Two young men in black leather stood, legs crossed, talking with one another, their fists closed around the black spikes of the fence as if impaled there. One kept a terrier on a lead at his heels. *What do they know?*

In Helen's study Krista sat very still. The small clock on the mantle ticked loudly and she waited. *The lie. Where was it?* She made a pledge to herself, to find those words if it took all night, all the next day, all next week, forever. They were in this study. That much she was certain of. She played with a cigarette, switched a plastic lighter on and off. *The words, where are they?* She finally lit the cigarette and allowed her eyes to slowly and carefully brush the spines of the neatly ordered shelves.

My mother's library. Those words are here. Krista felt confident of it. She would find what she was looking for. As she read the titles on the many books, she wondered if one might intuit the story of another's life by the books they read. She ran her eyes over the bookshelves, recognizing the leather-bound spines of her father's classics, their titles blocked in gold. Two books had shifted slightly, leaning to the right: *Stories from Hans Christian Andersen* and *Salome.* They in turn leaned against *Tales of Mystery and Imagination*, Edgar A. Poe. *The Outsider* rested heavily against *Peter Pan in Kensington Gardens, Robinson Crusoe, The Tempest, Rip Van Winkle, Don Juan, Candide,* and *Sinbad the Sailor.*

Krista read the titles faster. *The words, the lie. They are here somewhere.* Titles jumped off the shelves: *Moscow, Propaganda Man, The Future of Belief, The Decline of the Wasp, The Limits of Earth, The Passions of the Mind, Science and the Modern World, The Creative Process.*

The nausea returned. Words seemed to spin before her. The shelves appeared to be about to fall in on her. She saw the ceiling, the black scarring. She felt defeated and rested her head on the desk as she watched a cigarette in the ashtray burn slowly down to its filter. Suddenly, she got up, put out the cigarette, walked over to the wall of books. A dark leather-bound volume from the corner of the room where the shelves seemed less disturbed caught her attention.

"*East of the Sun and West of the Moon,*" Krista read aloud, as if acknowledging an old friend from long ago and far away. She drew her fingers, then her palm, over the front cover of the book, then opened it. There, penned in dark midnight blue, was Ilsa Bourne's graceful handwriting:

> *To my son, my little one, Charles:*
>
> *You, my Little Prince, will go to places of which I have only dreamt, just as your children will go to places of which you will only dream.*
>
> *Go with my blessings, and always remember to send them with yours.*
>
> *Love,*
> *Mother*
> *Christmas 1930*

Krista repeated the words to herself: "Love, Mother."

Love Mother. If only she could.

She leafed through the book of fairy tales with its fair-haired princes and princesses. Krista almost buckled under the overwhelming desire she felt then. She wanted to be back with Grandmother Bourne, with Ilsa. She needed her. She thought of the old whaling captain's house on the Vineyard, her grandmother's home. Krista suddenly needed her summer retreat more than she had ever needed anything before. As she sat in Helen's high-backed chair she reflected on her grandmother's paintings. The colors were luminescent, reminding her of daybreak on the Island, light spilling across the harbor as the first ferry pulled into port and the gulls squawked.

Krista recalled one painting in particular. It was a favorite of hers, though she had not considered it since Ilsa's death. She wondered if it were still hanging over the mantle in the summer house's parlor. It was one of the few landscapes her grandmother had painted. In it the season was not clearly indicated. Krista had often asked her grandmother if it was summer turning into fall or winter turning into spring.

Ilsa always said, "You must look for yourself. You must tell me."

Krista wanted the holiday magic Grandmother Bourne created. There was not a home like Ilsa's when the season called for food, gifts or sleeping under heavy blankets scented with last summer's wild roses. Krista could still remember her first Island Christmas. Clearly she recalled the fir tree placed in the corner of the parlor, touching the ceiling. A cascade of revolving silver and blue baubles graced one branch after the next, and Krista particularly enjoyed their handmade treasure trove of seashells each dancing on a dangling golden thread. She and Ilsa had made them all.

She loved the nativity scene. Her grandmother told her stories about reindeers and Jesus. Stories she made up on the spot. Stories that would never be repeated. Krista listened diligently. The aroma of breads, pies and roasting turkey filled the house and spilled out through the slightly cracked windows to the garden below.

"Love, Mother," Krista read aloud.

She thumbed through the book, stroking the delicate drawings. It seemed only yesterday she first laid eyes on them. She pulled her hair behind her ears, lifted her eyes from the pastel plate of a long-haired, blond princess, riding on the back of a white bear, who was really a prince. As she looked up, recalling Ilsa's voice telling the tale to her in soft gliding tones, she suddenly spotted it.

… may feel a stitch, a slight cramp, nothing different than a bit of premenstrual discomfort. Perhaps some spotting… But all in all, painless.

There was the book, nestled between Helen's diary and her first attempt at a screenplay. Right beside the glass ashtray where Krista had stubbed out the cigarette was the book: *My Body My Body* in bold black letters on the jacket. A subtitle spelled out: *My Understanding.* Those sharp letters were exact and angular. On the jacket was a photograph. A bouquet of diverse women held hands and smiled for the camera. It appeared to be a great big party. Krista let her tears fall on the book. The image lost focus. She might have been the blond one in the corner.

This was it: the source of the lie. Krista detested the faces of the women on the book's cover. She focused all her anger and pain on those women. *A party?*

Krista flipped through the pages, remembering. It had been four years ago. She had been fifteen. Cosmos had arrived in February, a snow-white kitten for her birthday from Daddy Bourne and Ilsa. Helen arrived too late from class to celebrate. She had come home with an armload of books, saying to Krista, "This one, here, catch it," as she almost dropped it. "I wish I had the chance to read a book like this when I was your age. You know, you have all the advantages. I am serious, Krista. I want you to read this. For your birthday."

It was not the present Krista had asked for. She had wanted new *pointe* shoes, white ones. Why, she asked herself, do I need a book like this? *Useless.*

"It's time you started thinking about your life. Dance is only sinking you further into the female stereotype," Helen added, tapping the cover of the book for emphasis.

"Stereotype?" Krista asked. "What are you talking about?"

"Thin. Beautiful," her mother answered dismissively. "Setting yourself impossible standards."

"What are you talking about?"

"Honest information. Real information. What you need, and what you are not going to find anywhere else. The truth about abortion, rape, incest. Read it."

"I'm not interested."

"You should be."

"Why?"

"Krista, you are impossible!"

She grudgingly took the book, swore she would never read it and did not until an overnight guest found it on a shelf in the library. Together the two girls read extracts aloud to each other.

As she sat there, recognizing the book, Krista felt afraid to pick it up. Her feelings remained unchanged. She still found the women in the pictures incomprehensible, without physical grace or seemingly much concern for their appearance. She sensed the recent changes in her own body. In just a month of being pregnant and not dancing she'd suffered loss of muscle tone, but more than that she felt as if the core had been gouged from her. *Where did they write about that?*

She stopped turning the pages, recalling the months after her fifteenth birthday. She had worn a white leotard that summer. Her shoes were white and her body was tan. Her hair whipped the air as she turned with ever-greater precision. She liked to think she could stop on a dime or dance on the head of a pin. Her teacher had told her how much the audience loved her, how she thrilled them. That she had a real future as a dancer. "They come for blood," her teacher had said, "and you give them that." It was the one and only time a teacher had ever given her such heartfelt praise.

Krista recalled afterwards trying to share the precious moment with her mother. Helen's response had been predictably negative. *What was the use of beauty, that spiraling feeling of weightlessness and light, when a woman's foot was bound, mutilated by white satin shoes concealing a block of wood in their toes?* Helen raged on about how Ilsa Bourne would rue the day she ever convinced her granddaughter to dance. Until Ilsa's death, it was forever a bone of contention between them, a deep-seated grudge that had left both women nursing hurt feelings and things unsaid. Krista sat in her mother's chair, in her mother's study, thinking about that accolade from her old teacher, holding on to the beauty of it, and for a few minutes lost contact with the pain she had been carrying all afternoon.

"Maybe *that* is the use of beauty," she said aloud, "it makes us forget the bad stuff in life."

Beauty and forgetting. Why didn't someone write about that?

Krista read the text in front of her. She had the same questions now as she had had when she first read the book. *Why, if these women wanted to do something, didn't they just do it?* Krista did not understand then, and did not understand now, how this book could be so significant for her mother. *Had these women only just discovered they had vaginas? What was the point?*

She slowly turned the pages. There it was, the chapter: A Termination. She read slowly through the types, the various international methods, including the United States. She passed over all the safety information and the debates from the medical community and various religious communities. She stopped at Reasons Why.

There, reading further, Krista found the lie. She ran her fingers under the titles: After Intercourse without Protection—Three Days to 12 Weeks; Vacuum Suction:

> *… like a Hoover… same idea… vacuums the walls of the uterus… drawing it up, through and out the tube. Start to finish? Six minutes. May feel a stitch, a slight cramp, nothing different than a bit of premenstrual*

discomfort. Perhaps some spotting... But all in all, painless.

Painless. Krista reread the word in disbelief.

"Painless?" she said out loud. "If it is painless then what is this that I am feeling?"

She read further:

... seventy-two-hour convalescence... some bleeding may occur. Some patients require no recovery period.

Krista looked down at her blue jeans, soaked through with blood. *Some bleeding? Recovery? Why did they lie? Why didn't they tell the truth? The would-be mother dies. Simple. Short. Sweet. Abortion is death.*

Krista picked up her mother's lighter. She flicked it on, then off. She looked at the desk, the shelves, the night outside, and wondered what she might do now that she had found the lie. Who could she punish? Who would pay for their part in spreading a falsehood? Or was she just different from the majority? Did so many other women feel nothing that the authors of the book felt they could safely say that an abortion was painless? Why didn't Dr. Blackwell or the nurses warn her of all the possible after-effects? What could she do about this?

Nothing.

"Nothing," she said aloud to no one.

Her answer silently danced around the room, circling her, seeming to taunt her. Krista felt like a child lied to for her own good. She felt tricked. She felt horribly deceived.

As she lifted the right-hand corner of the page with the intention of ripping it from the book, she stopped. She had a better idea. She set the page on fire, holding her mother's lighter to the thin paper.

The right-hand corner illustration, where a precisely drawn instrument penetrated a free-floating vagina, held open with forceps, and sucked from the uterus an amniotic sac, went up in flame. She watched fire spread instantly as if devouring autumn leaves. The flames spread from one page to the next while Krista leaned back in her mother's chair with a vague sense of satisfaction until she realized the desk was beginning to burn. She jumped up then, holding the book with just the tips of her fingers upon the boards and ran into the bathroom. There she tossed it into the bathtub and watched as the entire volume went up in smoke. Sitting on the edge of the tub, she waited until the book's entire spine collapsed, leaving a thick trail of ash on the scorched enamel.

Krista went back to the library. She tossed every book her mother had insisted she read into the tub. Wildly, she pulled others from the shelves: *I Know Why the Caged Bird Sings, Fear of Flying, Life in the Iron Mills, The Feminine Mystique, The Women's Room.* She watched them all go up in smoke. As she opened the window, she realized she was crying. The neighbors, she thought, what would they think? She did not want anyone to call the police or the fire department. Quickly, she turned on both faucets in the tub and doused the flames.

When they had died Krista noted the silence. It seemed immense. Another abdominal cramp left her doubled over. No one left, she thought, no one left to hurt. Using the wall for support, she felt her way to her room. The black ceiling, she asked herself, did I do that? From the street she heard a shrill whistle. It was Michael's. Had he packed?

Michael.

"Taxi!" he shouted.

"Wait," Krista whispered. "Wait… please wait for me."

She started for the door, saw the stain on her trousers, the soot on his shirt, and stopped. "Wait, wait, wait," she repeated to herself like a mantra. In the hall closet, she reached for a coat, anything to throw over herself so she could run into the street, stop him and tell him she had lied: she still loved him. But an immediate pang of pain was so excruciating that it took her breath away. A different pain this time. She took her stinging hand out of the closet and stared at it in disbelief. She had sliced it open on the old splintered frame of a painting.

Krista willed the blood and the throbbing to stop, gripping the injured hand hard with the unharmed one. Then she pulled the frame from the closet. It was a watercolor painting of Ilsa Bourne's old house, the family's summer house, viewed from the garden. The brick chimneys, the trellis, the apple tree, the greens, the blues – it was all there. She dragged it into the kitchen. As she bound her injured hand in a tea towel, she regarded the canvas. Instantly, she knew exactly where it was she must go and precisely what she needed to do there.

6

Krista continued to kneel with one clenched hand supporting the painting. Balancing it across the tops of her knees, she noticed her own reflection in the glass, superimposed over Ilsa's pristine white clapboard whaling captain's house. Her hair fell to her thighs, caught beneath the frame. It seemed to flow past the front lawn, encompassing the familiar scene. Krista studied the house, the apple tree, the back garden. Then she looked at her own reflection: the open collar of the white silk shirt, the cuffs rolled to her elbows, her thin face. The eyes she could not see. She recalled the old childhood game of inside-out. How many years ago had she played that with Mary and Deirdre? A lifetime, she thought to herself.

Krista set the painting against the wall and walked to the kitchen sink, where she rinsed her hand again, wrapping it tightly in a linen towel. The bleeding had stopped. She felt her pulse pounding against the makeshift bandage. *Two Gs*, she recalled her father saying, *two Gs, Krissie. Two Gs*, she thought to herself, as she recalled how unbearably hot the cockpit had been, how tightly he had turned the plane, and how the sunlight bounced mercilessly off the massive expanse of sea below.

She felt herself grow hot as if she were still in the cockpit. Her scalp pricked. *I will not vomit*, she told herself.

When she felt strong enough she changed her clothes. She had only one intention: to reach the summer house. She still held the watercolor of Ilsa's house. The car, she remembered, she could use that. Wasn't it ready to go? Hadn't her mother said so?

She stepped out into the cool early morning and walked to the garage, still carrying the painting. The night attendant nodded as she passed him. The car was ready for the trip to Nova Scotia. *How perfectly convenient.* With her grandmother's painting propped up beside her on the front seat, Krista reversed the Toyota Corolla. When the nausea returned, along with the memory of the cockpit, she glanced at the painting. She imagined herself safe; thought about the apple tree, the back garden, the stairs, and every other detail she could recall from every single room in the house. The inventory kept something at bay – what, she was not sure. She pulled her abdomen up and in hard against her spine. She did not want to feel its horrible, deep emptiness.

The silver sedan was one of the few cars on the city streets at four in the morning. Krista had no difficulty driving despite her hand feeling mildly numb from the deep cut. She imagined the car as her partner. They danced together through the early morning and her very real contemplation of the desire to take her own life. She considered Ilsa, the painting of the house, and how it was really a self-portrait of her grandmother. *Silent and sweet with some unspoken mystery.* Krista recalled candy found on concealed shelves, the thumping in her grandmother's breast as she rested against it while Ilsa read aloud fairy tales from leather-bound books. Krista saw that heart as pumping life and energy into the house: turning on lights, drawing baths, setting tables or feeding dogs leftovers from holiday dinners.

Late-night pedestrians loitered on street corners with their radios blaring. Trucks stopped and started somewhere off in the distance. Krista could almost smell the brake fluid. She rolled down the window. She needed cool air. She needed to breathe. At 72nd Street she turned left and got on the West Side Highway. The Hudson River hugged the road, and the lights of Jersey City looked almost cheerful. This route was familiar to her. She had traveled it every summer for what seemed like forever, and while there was a new building here or a new service station there, it remained virtually unchanged.

How many times had she taken this same route in her mind? On a lazy day when she wanted to escape, she often chose to imagine herself on this very drive. She recalled summer journeys spent sleeping or dreaming all the way to Martha's Vineyard, listening to her parents chat about the Island, what was changing there, what was not. The sound of the car's engine always put Krista to sleep. Her parents complained about the drive and wished they could fly.

The George Washington Bridge loomed ahead. Krista turned onto the Cross Bronx, and headed for Highway

95. Once she was in Connecticut, the traffic dwindled to almost nothing and the road seemed to turn into a straight line, possibly traveling into infinity. Krista cried as she listened to Pete Seeger sing.

"Travelin'," she sang with him, "travelin' on empty, runnin' scared."

The stars were still out in abundance and, despite recognizing their beauty, the profundity of the moment, being alone with the wind in her hair, Krista found herself wanting to drive straight out into the twilight, lose herself there. She could just drive over the line onto the wrong side of the road into the next oncoming car or truck. It would be so easy, she thought. *No. Get to Ilsa's. Just get to Ilsa's. Don't think. Just drive.* At Providence, she went onto 195, then 28. Wood's Hole and the ferry would not be far away.

The seven o'clock ferry waited. Krista felt the blood still seeping into the crotch of her jeans as it had done intermittently for hours. Would it ever stop? *I'll bathe at Ilsa's*, she decided. She descended the paved knoll, paid the attendant. He motioned her forward. Not one car in front of her in the line. She rolled up the center aisle and stopped, pulling on the emergency brake. *Don't let anyone I know see me*, she prayed. Krista went above board, hoping to catch the last of the sunrise.

The drizzle she found did not surprise her; neither did the air, thick with humidity or its tang of salt. She loved every bit of this journey that brought her home. Gulls perched on cabinets inscribed LIFEBOATS, the lightweight deckchairs and the white mast. Other passengers stayed inside, sipping coffee or tea, eating an egg and bagel. Krista leaned over the rail. The mainland receded. She looked towards Martha's Vineyard, her grandmother's island. *Forty-five minutes.* The ferry carved heavily through the water, sending spray fanning out on either side of the hull. Fishing boats headed out to sea and a passing tug sounded. The ferry hooted a low-toned response.

Down the railing, a young man in a red windbreaker nodded to Krista. She smiled politely and walked to the other side of the boat. The water, the sky, the floor of the ferry – all grey – seemed to engulf her. *Just jump. Jump. No, get to Ilsa's.* Krista wished for hard, damp sand where she might walk and not leave a trail. She wanted to live without leaving a trace. She wanted to die without leaving a trace. She simply wanted to disappear. The young man followed her, leaning over the rail beside her.

"Misty morning," he said.

"Yes."

"Aren't you Charlie Bourne's granddaughter?"

"No, you're mistaken."

Krista walked away from him and sat down in a blue deckchair. He did not follow this time but shrugged, cupped his hands and lit a cigarette. *I just want to be left alone. Forever,* she told herself. Krista thought about Ilsa's house, closed up for two summers. It would not be just as she remembered it.

Her hair curled in the light rain and she dug her hands into the pockets of her jeans, willing the Island to appear. Vineyard Haven, or the Harbor as some called it, appeared on the horizon. Krista practically raced to her car and sat drumming the steering wheel as she waited impatiently to disembark. She was afraid to let anyone or anything get in the way of what she intended to do.

Because the ferry was all but empty, she was able to drive off quickly and without encountering anyone. She took a left at the top of the hill, not turning back to look at the ferry or the Islanders waiting for their early morning guests as she might once have done. She felt she had to hurry, as if someone was waiting for her at the summer house. Out of Vineyard Haven, Krista felt her anxiety lessen. She turned onto Lambert's Cove Road, and when she saw the familiar stone walls, slowed down to a crawl. She wanted to take it all in. There, on the right, past Seth's Pond, was the place she loved best. Krista could almost sense her grandmother's house, stark and white on the horizon, raise itself up in a sort of salute. The house was set back from the road and Krista enjoyed taking it all in: the widow's walk at roof level, the blue shutters, the gnarly old apple tree. She touched the painting riding beside her as if it were a friend. *Don't let anyone see me*, she begged, and left the engine running as she ran to open the garage doors. After parking the car carefully out of sight, she made sure to leave everything undisturbed. The old rake that had been leaning against the garage door was returned to its exact position, and the empty gravel drive did not hint at her presence.

Carrying nothing but Ilsa's painting, Krista made her way to the cellar door. *Be unlocked, be unlocked*, she urged, and was sure that it must be. It had always been left that way for very good reason. The Bourne family was notorious for losing keys and Martha's Vineyard was a safe place. Everyone knew everyone else. The lightness and relief she'd felt as she left the ferry dissipated. Her steps grew leaden on the brick walk. She hesitated on the pathway, stopped at the garden gate and stared at the wintry apple tree. *Ilsa is not here. Had I forgotten? What was I thinking? Hurry. Hurry. I will not lose courage. This is not about Ilsa. It's about me.* Krista lifted the weather-beaten green door, letting it swing closed behind her on its warped hinges. *Ilsa is not so far away.* She felt over the rough brick for the switch to the single bulb that hung from the basement's ceiling. She thought about the family graveyard not so far away, and of her grandmother's grave in particular, nestled beside her son's, Krista's father's grave, which remained empty.

Summer chairs, neatly lined up under a blue tarp, leaned against the wall. The bicycles Ilsa had called "the dinosaurs" blocked her path to the stairs. Krista stepped over them and passed the random shutters taken off a window here and a window there years ago with the idea of someday painting them. The gas water heater momentarily kicked on, and she froze as if she might not be alone.

"You scared me," she said out loud.

Krista felt her way up the steps. Old beach towels, robes, picnic baskets and plastic ice chests hung from the ceiling. She pushed open the basement door. The stale smell of the closed house enveloped her. The silence frightened her momentarily. Her footsteps echoed cavernously across the wooden floor. In the kitchen she expected to see Ilsa. *Grandmother is dead*, she reminded herself. Stepping out of her shoes she walked over to the back door, where the ivy, growing unchecked over the last few years, scratched against the screen in the morning wind. In the dining room she noticed her breath hanging in the air. *Was it that cold?* The shutters, which had always been crooked, hung at an even more dangerous angle. They might fall that very second. Someone had written his or her name in the dust on the stereo and the lid stood open on the piano. *Had Grandfather Bourne been here? When? Certainly not Helen.* Krista hit middle C and held the key down. In the empty house the sound seemed to reverberate forever. She drew her finger through the dust on the record albums then sat for a while in the alcove, staring at Ilsa's self-portrait.

The likeness seemed a little flat today. Krista did not see the customary iridescence in the handling of the paint that she recalled as her grandmother's signature. Curiosity got the better of her. She rose from the damp cushions. She passed Ilsa's bedroom, the place where her grandmother had died. Krista knew the room well: the wreath of dried summer flowers on the wall, the painted floor, the lambskin throws, the pink vanity, the endless photographs of family in their silver frames. All would be covered in dust. Too sad to contemplate.

In the study, she sat down on one of the rattan mats and shivered. She felt weightless, the only breath of warmth in a cold house. Ilsa's desk lay as it always had, covered in bills, letters, articles, and stock market reports. Old issues of *Fortune*, *Time*, *Business Week* and *The Wall*

Street Journal lay beside the chair that faced the television. From that chair she had monitored a world into which she never ventured.

Krista pulled the muslin dust covers from the living-room chairs and sat down. The front room was thick with the smell of smoke from the grate. Ash in the fireplace lay at least an inch deep. A draft stirred a small piece of paper from the grate. Krista considered her favorite painting hanging over the mantle. *Still there.*

"What season is it?" she asked aloud.

The shades were drawn. To Krista's recollection they had always been kept closed to give protection from the sun – or so Ilsa told her family. Again, Krista stood up; she was still carrying the watercolor she had carried with her from New York. She moved uneasily through the house. In the foyer, she stopped before the mirror and closed the neck of her blouse. *Who is this?* she wondered, studying her own reflection. *I don't recognize you.* She was more like a painting of a fragile girl than a flesh and blood one. Leaning on the banister, she mounted the steps, stopping only momentarily at the tight corner landing, crafted by a ship's carpenter. Curls of dust lifted underfoot.

In the front bedroom everything lay quiet and draped. Krista's fingertips felt extraordinarily cold as she turned the cut-crystal handle on the door. She drifted through Ilsa's studio, past the drafting board, the rows of paintings in progress, the cans full of brushes, the paints dried in their tubes and the wooden screen with the dancing Indian goddess decorating it. A light rain beat against the skylight and a trickle found its way through. It tapped against a large piece of plastic covering a small hand-painted chair.

The next room had been Krista's summer bedroom. The walls were painted yellow, and there was a framed picture of a small fleet of fishing boats bobbing in a calm harbor at sunset. Krista looked again at the watercolor of Ilsa's house. *What was it?* She propped it against the wall, and lay down on the four-poster bed in which her father had been born. *What was it?*

She pulled her arms in tightly and cupped her wounded hand in the good one, pressed together over her heart. Turning towards the wall, she smelled the musty pillow. She felt stiff and sore. Opening her eyes, she smiled. There directly before her was the prayer she had recited with her father. It was framed in driftwood and printed under a drawing of the morning star. She closed her eyes and recited:

"Now I lay me down to sleep
I pray The Lord my soul to keep,
Thy love be with me through the night,
And bless me with the morning light."

Blood dried on the insides of her thighs and along the seams of her jeans. The house stayed as still as if no one had arrived and no one would leave, as perhaps they would not. Krista still intended to die here.

7

Krista lay unable to sleep. Fatigue played all sorts of games on her except the one she most wanted: sleep. The pervasive cold convinced her she might be on her way to dying. She recalled that someone once told her life withdraws slowly, first from the fingertips, then the toes. It recedes up the insides of the arms and the legs. The extremities grow cold first, then numb. That was the way a person might freeze to death from exposure.

I just want to die. Is that too much to ask?

"So kill yourself," she thought she heard someone say.

Kill myself?

"Precisely."

How?

"There are any number of ways."

Any number of ways?

"Any number."

I could slit my wrists.

"Too messy."

In the bathtub?

"How prosaic."

Or hold my breath.

"Ridiculous!"

Drown.

"A possibility."

Overdose.

"No drugs, please."

Gas.

"Not a bad idea."

The oven maybe.

"No, the car."

The car.

"Or you could always starve yourself."

Starve myself? Stay here. Stay here on the Island. Stay here like Ilsa for the rest of my life.

"There you go. Now you're making sense."

"Stop!" she shouted to the voice she could not quite make out. "Stop." The house was empty and she knew it would be a while before anyone figured out where she was hiding.

She rolled over but did not fall asleep. She rested in a sort of suspended wakefulness, feeling her heart pound. She allowed herself to curl up around the steady pounding, the vestigial source of heat. The sound of it seemed incredibly loud, almost deafening. She imagined the valves opening and closing. The pounding turned into the sound of hooves, an easy gallop over frozen ground. She saw marsh hay open in front of her and close behind.

Where could I ride?

"To the edge of the world, my darling. To the edge of the world."

Krista opened her hand ever so slightly and held it out as if her grandmother were sitting right there beside her.

"You will not die, my precious darling. You are too strong for that. I know because I was too weak. You will not take your own life. All of this is valuable."

"Ilsa?" Krista asked aloud, knowing no one was there.

She thought of her grandmother and the bed grew warm. She smelled the old days. Baking. Apple pie made with green apples, cinnamon and raisins. She started to cry. *Where are you when I need you? What do I do now? I hurt. I want my baby back. I want my body back. My life back. Nobody told me how much it would hurt.*

She sensed Ilsa curling around her cold body and let go. She rocked a little. What were the first things she always noticed about Ilsa? Her Lily-of-the-Valley scent for one. The soft folds in her dewy white skin. And her hands, strong and deft. Hands that could paint anything, and grow a garden that was second to none.

What else could she recall? Lying on her tummy in the garden. The smell of grass. Dark earth. Ladybirds. Cold toes and Ilsa humming while she raked. The bells that jingled on the garden gate.

And love. I recall love.

The memories rolled by one after the other, from bubble baths using her grandmother's prized French bottle to orchids for the prom. When had Ilsa not been there for her? Krista rolled over and pulled the neck of her jersey up to her chin. *God, I loved her so much. What didn't she teach me about bad stuff? What would she do now?*

She would get up. She would count her blessings, Krista told herself. *Blessings? What blessings?* No career, no husband, no father, no mother for all practical purposes, no child, no sisters, no brothers, nowhere to live except Grandfather's home.

"But I had a grandmother," she said aloud. "I once had a grandmother."

"You have a grandmother," she thought she heard someone whisper. "I might be dead, but I am here with you always. Didn't I tell you: forever and always? Love is forever and always. Eternal. Yes, from beyond the grave. Now let's begin somewhere. Remember?"

"I remember."

"Okay then, let's go."

"Ten fingers, ten toes."

"Ten fingers, ten toes."

"A nose. I can smell."

"Eyes. I can see."

"Beautiful eyes. Unlike any others."

"Thank you."

"And hands."

"And hands, with which to pray."

"And gratitude."

"And gratitude. I love you."

"I love you, too. Now count the things you're grateful for."

"Nothing beyond you, Grandmother."

"Think harder, darling. Think harder."

"There's nothing." Krista drew a blank. She rubbed her hands together and cupped her knees. "Father?"

"Yes," she supposed Ilsa would say. "Yes, you have a father."

"A dead one."

"A dead one, who was once alive."

"Who was once alive." Krista tried to recall his face and could not, but she could feel him. Curly hair, she recalled. Tobacco. Warmth. She felt her own toes. *My father. Without whom I would not be.*

"Without whom you would not be. You miss him as much as I did."

"No. I never knew him."

"You knew him."

"How could I? I was only three when he died."

"Krista, what do you miss?"

"The idea of him, of what I might have had."

"Krista, what do you miss?"

"Him, Ilsa, him."

"Krista."

"Love, Ilsa. I miss love, and him, and you."

"So now we are counting. Fingers, toes, your father."

"You, and love."

"There is always love, Krista."

"But what's the point? You're dead, he's dead."

"Helen is still alive."

"My mother?" Krista nearly shrieked.

"Your mother."

Krista went numb again. The voice faded away. Mother, she repeated herself. *Mother.* The anger and pain were so great.

"I hate my mother," she shouted out loud, "put *that* on your list."

The house grew cold again. The wind picked up. Fear crept over her when she thought she heard someone downstairs, heard the basement door open and close. Maybe it was a loose shutter.

"Fingers and toes, fingers and toes," she whispered.

"That's better," the voice soothed her.

"I still hate Mother."

"Okay. Is there anything you like about her?"

"No."

"So, die."

"I want to."

"Do you?"

"No."

"Then live."

"How?"

"By being grateful."

"For what?"

"Everything, Krista. Everything. Including your mother."

"She's done nothing for me. This abortion was *her* fault. She believes in all that stuff – the right to choose."

"Love her for giving you life."

"I can't."

"You can."

"It was an accident. *I* was an accident. As she never tires of telling me."

"Maybe, but she brought you into this life. If nothing else, be grateful for that."

Life. I could be grateful for that.

Krista fell into a deep sleep, and did not awake until the street lamp outside shone through the crack in the curtains and on to her bed. Her first waking thought was of the painting over the mantle in the parlor below. *What season was it?* She felt a small tug, almost as if Ilsa were urging her out of bed, the way she had when Krista was a child.

"Get up! Wake up, sleepyhead."

8

Krista pulled back the drapes, snapped up the blind and opened the window. Shocked by the cold air, she was no less astonished to find that it was not twilight outside, not even sunrise. It was no street lamp that had woken her. It was about ten o'clock in a clear, bright mid-morning. She had slept the day away yesterday, which made it… What day? And then she remembered – September 21st. A rush of joy swept through her at the official beginning of fall, her favorite time of year. Overhead gulls squawked. Feeling the pull of the equinox, the tide churned against the shore beyond the back pasture, the meadow at the hem of the marsh.

Below her in the overgrown yard she counted twenty-seven apples; no fruit remained on the boughs. One branch had split away from the trunk and lay touching the ground. Far out on the horizon a ship's funnel reflected the sun. Ilsa's house. Krista could not imagine a better view.

She turned from the window. The bloodstain centered on the white tufted bedspread frightened her for an instant, until the past few days' events came back, one by one. She touched her belly, finding it tight with hunger. And, oddly, when she thought of the life that had been growing there so recently, she felt a great relief that it was there no longer. Her lethargy and sense of disconnection had disappeared. She pulled the spread from the bed, thinking to launder it. Dust rose from the dresser and nightstand, and she brushed against the prayer tacked to the wall. Smiling, she remembered evenings kneeling at the side of this four-poster bed, saying prayers with Ilsa, blessing everyone, everything, delaying bedtime by one detail after the next. On the dresser was a balsa-wood whale. The blue jay feather she had stuck in its blowhole years ago – so many years that the whale would hardly appear the same without it – waved in the breeze through the open window. And there was the shell, the white scallop shell, her father's legacy to her that she had kept for him all these years.

Looking in the mirror, she shook her head at her reflection. A mess. Her hair seemed to be matted, resisting all attempts to comb it with her fingers, Michael's shirt, bloodied, hung from below her sweater, and her jeans were hard-crusted with blood. She stripped herself and bundled the clothes together to dispose of. Shivering, she ran to the bathroom, lifting Ilsa's musty old wool robe from the back of the door. Water flowed brown at first from the faucet, then thankfully clear.

Before taking her bath, she turned on the kitchen stove, leaving the door open so as to warm the room. It seemed too cold for September but the house had been closed up for so long – no light, no air. Fall, the first day – it had been a month since her last dance class. She recalled Madame Chevalier's ultimatum. "Not until you can bring me life. A full extension," she mimicked, rising upon both feet in *relevé*, going into *plié*, lifting her leg in *arabesque*. "A full extension yourself," she said, prancing back up the steps to the back room. Krista rolled her head, rolled her shoulders, and bent each vertebra in her spine until she was touching her palms to the floor.

She let the water run in the kitchen sink until the rust had cleared, rummaging in the closets meanwhile for something she might wear. None of her old things fit so she stole into her grandmother's studio where she found a pair of jeans, so old the denim felt like flannel. She found a work shirt covered with splatters of dry paint, mostly white and yellow. After digging in a few more drawers, she decided to go without underwear. The bathtub was full, almost overflowing. From the linen closet she took a washcloth smelling of mothballs. An old box of tampons was inadvertently knocked to the floor and Krista retrieved it, amazed. How long had these been around? The carton looked like an old ad for war bonds.

The water closed over her, up to her chin in the deep old tub. She squeezed water over her arms, rinsed her face, and dipped her head back into the water, wringing her hair over her shoulder. She pinned it up with Ilsa's combs, always left by the side of the tub, to the top of her head. The dried blood on her thighs loosened and dissolved. Everything seemed to have a new significance. Even the soap – a two-year-old bar of Ivory, half worn down – seemed precious. Krista scrubbed between her toes, stretching the backs of her thighs. She attributed her joy to not being pregnant and to being back in her grandmother's house.

Or to life maybe.

She pumiced her knees, the backs of her elbows, her heels, and the calluses on the soles of her feet.

"Never," she said aloud, "never, never, never. I will never dance again." She cracked the joints of each toe and then wondered what she might do instead. She didn't know. She poured water over each shoulder.

What would she do? She refused to go back to New York, or even to think about Michael. The heated water lulled her until she recalled the voice yesterday. Ilsa's voice. *Was it a dream?* Something or someone had urged her to look at the painting over the mantle, and had they suggested she remain in the summer house? *It's a great idea. I will stay here. I will reopen the summer place*, she decided.

Filled with an unfamiliar zest and vigor, Krista knew exactly what she would do next. She would become an Islander. She would live the way her grandmother had lived; emulate the woman she loved more than any other. She would wake up every morning to bathe with Ivory soap, put on a pair of old flannel jeans, then paint or write. Or maybe she'd just ride horses. She would have this house to herself. Daddy Bourne would be thrilled to see it reopened, especially by Krista. *On my own. I would love to be on my own.*

"As for Michael," she said aloud, shrugging her shoulders then toweling them dry, "I ended that."

Krista pulled on Ilsa's side-buttoned jeans and promenaded before the mirror. *How long ago had these been in vogue? If they ever had been at all.* She rolled her shirt cuffs to the elbow and turned the collar up, leaving the tails to hang. *Just like Ilsa did.* She slipped into an old pair of Dr. Scholl sandals, rinsed the tub, the sink, and pushed back the pink half-curtains before sliding open the window. Again, the chill outside surprised her.

The air was fresh and opening all the windows became Krista's first step in her new plan to become an Islander. In front of the stove she changed her mind, however. She was hungry. The windows could wait until the afternoon. Famished, she turned towards the refrigerator only to be disappointed. The door stood ajar, the light out and the shelves empty, except for a sad-looking box of baking soda. The cupboards held not much more: stale cereal, outdated envelopes of spices, rusted cans of beans, ravioli and palm hearts. *Nothing appetizing.* Then from behind an old box of cake frosting well past its sell-by date, Krista noticed a familiar green wrapper. Semi-sweet German chocolate. *How many times did I practically get on my knees for this?*

Krista laughed as she found the use-by date. *Two years old.* She broke the seal on the wrapper and opened the package. *Could I die from eating two-year-old chocolate?* The candy tasted delicious. Krista took it into the dining room where she opened the shutters and closed the piano lid, only to notice the dust. *Perhaps I should start with dusting.*

From the shopping bag behind the cellar door, Krista took a dust rag and wiped the piano, then the old hi-fi components. She lightly brushed over the collection of LPs and then the table, tossing the dry flowers into the kitchen sink. She dusted the buffet and remembered the chandeliers. In the dining-room closet she found the silver, the china and the vacuum cleaner.

In the study she tossed old magazines and newspapers into a pile. She munched on the chocolate from time to time, stashing it in her shirt pocket. The stereo blared and she danced to hits from her grandparents' era as she dusted and generally straightened things up. In the living room she pulled the muslin drapes from the furniture and snapped open the blinds. She sat down in Ilsa's reading chair at last, feeling tired but happy. She had already made a small difference.

Krista pressed the spines of the books evenly into place on the bookshelves with the palm of her hand. On the side table she shifted two glass tigers and rang a 1976 Liberty Bell. Impulsively, she rolled a newspaper and placed it in the fireplace, lit kindling, and put the one remaining log in the basket against the back of the grate. The fire caught easily and she knelt back on her heels, recalling for an instant burning her mother's books in the apartment. It seemed ages ago. *When would they show up? Soon, but not right now.* Again she rang the small bell and replaced it on the table, picking up the diary that lay there. It was a simple journal, one of the many dotted around the house, containing roughs, ideas and the odd note regarding maintenance, repair and ferry schedules. Sometimes they included the odd poem-like sketch.

Turning the pages Krista heard Ilsa, just two summers ago, saying, "Be organized, Darling, be organized, but not too much. We really don't know much more than what happens in one day, never mind forever. Love for now.

Love for this twenty-four hours. Live for this twenty-four hours. That's enough." Krista was not thinking about being organized now or forever; loving now or forever. She flipped through the journal, recalling the way her grandmother read aloud, as if the voice came not from her lips but directly from her heart. Krista hugged the small journal to her chest, listened to the crackling of the log on the fire, and told her grandmother as if it had been her suggestion, "You're right, I'll stay here. I'll stay right here. I'll be an Islander. Like you."

Returning to Ilsa's daily planner, a full schedule, an agenda Krista never really knew existed, Krista imagined Ilsa's days. The fire sputtered. She found a long, hastily scribbled, poem-like outline erased here and crossed out there, written on a Saturday. It appeared to be Ilsa's love affair with Morning, Noon and Night. For an instant, Krista heard something upstairs and felt frightened, only to realize the wind had whipped the curtains against the wall in the bathroom and her bedroom. The hall door slammed. Krista recalled her dream from the previous evening. She heard Ilsa's voice say: "You will not kill yourself."

She clutched the cloth-bound volume to her chest and listened. The wind filled the house as breath might fill a body. Continuing to read, Krista visualized Ilsa somewhere, sometime, between running errands, swimming, paying bills, painting, taking time, perhaps right here in this very chair to jot down a bit of beauty, an idle thought. Ilsa was like that, brimming with good, innocence. Krista savored the words between the smudges and erasures.

"Sunrise, meet Day, who has come to stay,
I won't say for always."
Even if Morning feels that way.
Minutes tick slowly.
More time.
I create.
Despite that, Love and Day rush by.
Into birdsong, eternal.
Morning turns forever into Noon and into Night.
Noon, a better bedfellow, bold and bright.
What will I ever tell Night?
While Noon, my hearty companion, lingers;
Eventually, all three loves slip away.
Love and Life and Loss.
Morning, Noon and Night.
The clock ticks, the hands turn.
Birdsong.
"Not forever," Night chides.
"Only one day at a time," he explains.
Morning, Noon and Night.
Nothing lasts forever,
Except this one, Sweet Moment.
This Shasta Daisy, this Montblanc fountain pen, this
rake in my hand, the falling McIntosh fruit…

Krista closed her eyes. She kept one finger inserted in the diary to hold her page.

"Nothing lasts forever, except this one, Sweet Moment… only… the Shasta Daisy, the falling McIntosh fruit."

She repeated the lines as she watched her small fire die. She rested her chin on the book. *Except this one, Sweet Moment.* She recalled the twenty-seven McIntosh apples on the ground beneath the ancient tree, the one limb hanging down. A cool draft blew an ember from the fire, which Krista quickly kicked back into the hearth.

Picking up Ilsa's diary again she fumbled to find the page she had been reading. *What was Ilsa saying?* Krista thought of her sweet grandmother who always took the ordinary and raised it up to something special, sweet and redeeming. *So innocent.* As she flipped through the diary she discovered instead an extra page, not like the others, wedged between the bound ones. The edges were tattered and the paper lightweight. She pulled it out. Two sheets of notebook paper were folded in half and four times across. They bore Ilsa's handwriting. In some places the ink ran. There were two circular water stains, one in the center of the dark script. Other than that the lettering was steady, consistent, the marks evenly pressed except for the crossing of the Ts.

Those letters began as if pressed firmly then disappeared as they angled upwards. Krista read the note as lazily as she savored the remainder of the bar of chocolate:

This is where I remember fear, pure physical fear. Fear of surgical instruments, the furtive faces, and, of course, blood. If I were to paint an abstraction of that hole-in-the-wall place, it would contain black, white, steel grey and naturally red. Buckets of red. However, it was over very quickly, physical pain was kept at a minimum. The cost was high.

The relief is tremendous. But the guilt, for curtailing a life, has hung on a lifetime, my constant companion. My warden. There was a feeling of being defiled, but I believed that stemmed from the sordidness of the surroundings, that dark hole on the Upper West Side. I don't think the defilement, the guilt, would have occurred if the operation had not been illegal. This I will never know for sure.

But this painting, I cannot paint. This is the painting in which I live. This house. This Island. This canvas.

It ended abruptly. Krista read it again in disbelief. This randomly found note had appeared at first just like the others Ilsa left here and there: in drawers, in books, in smock pockets. They usually contained ideas for paintings, schemes for the garden, plans for a renovation or a holiday ornament.

Krista tried to imagine her grandmother's note as purely a sketch for a painting. She considered the canvas it might have produced. *I have never seen this painting.* The colors did not ring true. The possibilities were unlike anything her grandmother had ever painted. Krista focused on the landscape above the mantle and heard her grandmother tease her: "You tell me, Krissie, you tell me what season it is."

I don't know.

The shoreline wavered around a brilliant green knoll, which in turn supported a lone tree with a rough trunk, its branches raised high into the sky. There, for the first time, Krista saw steel grey, a surgical shade of steel grey, dominate. *It wasn't a question of sunset or sunrise, spring or fall.* Beyond the iridescence Krista always saw in Ilsa's paintings, she now saw a sweeping, distinct crescent of red, the color of blood, cut into the canvas, deftly bordered by sweeps of amber. The traces of black, white, steel grey and red became paramount, and again she heard Ilsa say, "You tell me, Krissie, you tell me what season it is."

Krista read the note again. *Ilsa had an abortion. An illegal abortion.* When? Where? The questions raced through her mind. The Upper West Side, a dark hole. It had hurt; she had felt guilty. Krista seemed to hear every door in the house lock. Upstairs a door slammed again.

"No," she said aloud.

I am not guilty. I am not hurt. I am choosing to live here as Ilsa did: because she wanted to, because she loved the Island. She was an artist. She was not guilty, not hurt. I knew my grandmother.

Krista stared at the painting, the darkness she had never seen in it before. In the hall, a vacuum cleaner leaned against a set of golf clubs. The dust rag rested on the pile of papers and magazines where she had left it. In the dining room, the candlesticks stood in the wrong place on the wrong table. The cellar door was ajar. Pieces of torn linen hung from the shopping bag.

My abortion was legal. I am not guilty. It is not a sin. I did not commit a crime.

She considered the choice she had had, unlike her grandmother. *But I felt the same. I too curtailed a life.*

She felt yesterday's nausea come back. She understood her fear, her power. It was one she felt a man could never understand. An authority beyond legislation.

I will stay.

Krista picked up the dust rag. *Maybe this is a sort of penance. Maybe like Ilsa…*

Upstairs a window slammed. Krista heard the brief ticking of a clock that for some reason loosened the last spiral in its spring. *My fate is sealed. I will remain here, forever, in the summer house, keeping her secret and mine.*

The aftertaste of chocolate in her mouth was bitter. For the first time, she understood Ilsa's paintings. Her depictions were gay, full of beauty, but rich only because of the under painting, the colors that, once seen, cut like a knife.

"You tell me," Krista said out loud, "you tell me what season it is."

So that was the reason, she thought, that was the reason I felt Ilsa so close, as if she were sitting on my bed, chiding me in that way she always had. Krista held the folded note in one hand as she blew dust off the mantelpiece. She noticed that the cut in her palm still stung, and watched the small, dark shadows from the glazing bars in the windowpanes dance on the living-room floor. She felt guilt, her own and Ilsa's. The house no longer seemed a joyful place, a haven. To stay here did not feel like a choice. *The summer house will be the price I pay. I curtailed a life, Ilsa curtailed a life. We are criminals. Who really has the right to take a life?*

"God," she said out loud, "and men at war."

Krista wept. She sat on the hearth, and for the first time had a clear sense of her power to create and destroy. She felt inadequate and afraid. *Was it wrong to give women the right of God?* She imagined what it might be like if not one unloved child were born into the world, if a woman were never to suffer for her decision, and if people were not afraid of death. Even if, she thought, the question of the maimed, the crippled and the sick were left aside, and just the unloved children aborted – what would that mean? What if no unloved child would be born into that sort of poverty? How would the world change?

Ivy scratched at the front door. Tires crunched the gravel in the driveway, and the quick setting of an emergency brake preceded footsteps hurrying up the brick path. The bells under the arch covered with Baltic ivy rang, and someone pounded heavily on the kitchen door.

"Krista," Michael's voice demanded, "are you there?"

9

Michael continued to knock and to rattle the latched screen door. Krista dropped the dust cloth to the floor, stepped out of her wooden-soled sandals, and moved towards the foyer, then up the carpeted stairs. *He mustn't know I'm here. I'm not ready to talk to him*, she decided. First she considered the airing cupboard, where the winter blankets now remained all year, then the steamer with its piles of old tea towels and satin quilts, but the key was missing and the lid locked tightly into place. She considered the fireplace in Ilsa's studio, behind the screen. Looking up, she saw a charcoal sketch, one of her father's first drawings, guided by the hand of a young Ilsa.

"Dad, Ilsa… help me," Krista whispered. "I don't want him here. I don't want him to find me."

She eyed her bed. The height of the frame from the floor was too low. The banging on the back door stopped, only to resume at the front, even louder than before. Krista remembered the cellar door. It was not latched. Could she make it down there before he discovered it?

"Krista, open the door!" Michael shouted.

She held still.

"Kris, listen to me," he pleaded

She looked at the stripped bed. *Not here.*

The bathroom? The linen closet? Krista wanted only to disappear. She guessed he had already seen the car in the garage. *How else could he know? Perhaps the open blinds and windows.* Back in the studio, she rested her hand on a large empty frame. As Michael continued to pound the doors and call out, she spotted the tall Indian screen that concealed the door to a low-ceilinged attic room beyond, the one in which Ilsa's paintings were stored along with some old books and an ancient baby carriage. Krista recalled the stuffy space in which on many a summer afternoon she hid from Ilsa, saved from taking a nap, only to fall asleep there beside a china doll whose eyes opened and closed depending on whether she was sitting or lying down. Krista stepped behind the screen, lifted the sagging door carefully, and hid in the space behind.

"Kris, I know you're in there. I don't want anything from you... just to know you're okay."

"I'm okay," she said under her breath, settling back against a large easel. She realized she still held Ilsa's note, and pressed it to her lips. *Michael, please, please, please, just go away.*

The knocking continued. If anything, it increased in volume. Michael was now at the back door again, standing immediately by the cellar entrance. If she peered out the tiny attic window, she knew she would be able to see him. She crawled to it, knocking over a coffee tin full of brushes, which she stopped from rolling with her heel. She watched him. He pounded twice, called out her name, a despairing expression on his face.

He slumped down on the cement stoop, resting his forearms on his knees. "Kris!" he called up to the attic window.

She quickly backed away. *Did he see me?*

"Kris, open the door. You are out of your mind. Open the door."

He slammed his fist against the cellar door in frustration. The blow reverberated through the house. The door swung in slightly under the blow, and he stared at it. In seconds, Krista could hear the creaking of the hinges as he found the way in. She closed her eyes and scooted to the far corner of the attic, pushing the baby carriage in front of the door.

In the basement, Michael knocked over a bicycle and tripped on the stairwell. His voice reached her, muffled by the floorboards that separated them. "Kris, this is crazy! I know you're here. Please answer me. Just tell me you're okay."

"Ilsa, please," Krista prayed, "send him away."

As soon as she said the little prayer, she felt enormously safe. Krista did not understand how Ilsa could do it, but she knew Michael would not come poking about upstairs. He would not go that far, she was certain, and relaxed, deciding it was only a matter of staying very still until he gave up and left. Again, she leaned against the easel, guessing where he was by his voice and the different sounds of his footsteps, on the carpeting or the hardwood floors.

Michael dialed the phone. Krista jumped, catching the familiar sound. *Wasn't the phone dead? Hopefully...* It was not. Just as the water and the gas and the electricity had never been cut off, so the phone had remained ready for use.

She heard Michael say, "Mr. Bourne, please."

What right does he have to call my grandfather? she thought angrily while he waited to be put through. *Maybe this is a trick.* She remained still.

"She's here." Michael paused. "No. The cellar door's unlocked. The stereo's warm. There's been a fire in the front room. I found a pair of sandals... I don't feel comfortable being here. I don't want to dig around. If she doesn't want to see anyone this might not be a good idea."

Krista listened.

"All right," Michael continued. "Did you get a hold of Helen? I'll keep looking." He hung up.

The house fell silent for a moment only to echo to Michael's steps on the front stairwell. He was directly under Krista. She was surprised he couldn't hear her heart beating.

"Krista." He slugged the bedroom door and rattled the knob on the locked storage closet in the front room. He made his way through the bathroom and bedroom. Krista remembered the bedspread on the floor, her clothes in the bathroom.

It doesn't matter. So what if he knows I am here or that I have been here? He knows nothing else, and until we are face to face, he can know nothing for sure. I just do not want to confront him, nothing else matters. I do not want to confront him.

The closet door in her room opened and closed. The footsteps approached the Indian screen, stopped, and turned away. Michael flipped through a sketchpad, the pages sounding one after the next. "Your grandmother was pretty good," he announced. "All right," he said, sighing aloud, "I give up. Have it your way, but I know you're here." And he kicked the Indian screen so hard that it toppled over, leaning against the door to the attic room. "Have it your way."

He walked out the front bedroom, down the stairs to the kitchen. Krista kept still, clutching Ilsa's note in her hand. She started to go after him, and pushed against the door, but the toppled screen prevented her from getting out. She could not call out to him. Something prevented her. Despite herself, the call for help caught in her throat.

He halted in the dining room, again raising his voice to call to her. "You think I'm stupid? You think I didn't see the car in the garage? You're written all over this place, but I'm not going to smoke you out. You can come after me when you're good and ready. Did you hear me? I am not coming back."

He unlocked the kitchen door and let himself out. The door slammed shut again. Krista listened to his steps on the gravel, the car door banging, and the engine noise as he backed out of the driveway.

She pushed against the door. It remained closed. She sat back down, still holding the note. The house settled, bird-like, after the recent incursion, as if smoothing ruffled feathers. She started to cry, and then, as there was no reason to restrain herself, broke into wailing sobs.

After some time, Krista stopped. She listened. The silence was deafening. This time there was no Ilsa coming to retrieve her, no Ilsa coming to admonish her for hiding, or for sleeping in the attic instead of in her own bed, no Ilsa coming to say, "Next time, young lady..."

Ilsa was dead. Her son was dead. Krista repeated those words to herself. *No one is coming.* Suddenly she was very sure. Neither Daddy nor Ilsa would walk back into her life. She had always half expected her father to walk back in, somehow, somewhere. She had been waiting forever. And Ilsa? She saw the bronze coffin lowered into the grave, smelled the fresh, upturned earth. She had been to the graveyard innumerable times. *But wasn't there a possibility? Couldn't the past ever come back?* Krista placed her hands on her abdomen. She had her answer.

They will never come back. They are gone. Dead. I have tried to keep them alive by holding onto the past, by denying life as it proceeded. And now I am doing the same thing with this tiny spirit I have had with me for the past four weeks. Am I going to hold onto that for years, the way I have with Ilsa and ever since Daddy disappeared?

"They can – they can come back," she said out loud, defiantly.

She reached for the note she'd found earlier and tore it into pieces. "No!" she shouted into the yawning silence. There was no one to agree or disagree with her, just emptiness.

"Yes."

Daddy and Ilsa are gone. My baby is gone. They are dead.

Krista threw herself against the jammed door and the silence in which she did not want to die. The Indian screen with the inlaid pattern of a many-armed dancing goddess fell away, toppling over a drafting board and dislodging a table lamp. Krista ran down the back steps to the cold kitchen. She opened the door and stood for a minute looking out the gate towards the garage, then at the back path, the meadow and the marsh.

Michael, where are you?

There was no sign of his car. No sign that anyone had been here. Had she merely dreamed that he had come to the house? No, she told herself. Michael had come. He had asked her to come out. He had come to see if she was all right. He was no dream, no illusion, but flesh and blood.

The small bell on the garden gate tinkled as she opened it and hurried down the long driveway, underneath the grapevine-covered arbor. She ran barefoot to the main road. There was no sign of him. She looked up and down the street, then turned back towards the house. Unexpectedly, she found it did not matter to her whether or not it had been a dream. The only thing that mattered to Krista in that moment was the sun. The light and heat spilling across the open marshes, the garden, the apple tree, and over her face, her arms, her legs… bringing her back to life.

10

The sound of a hammer rang out, echoing through the oak grove that formed the boundary between the Bourne property and the one next door. The neighbor's house was being boarded for the off-season. *Did that mean Deirdre or her mother might still be home supervising?* Krista ran back into her grandmother's house and slipped on her shoes. She took the back gate and the path along the fieldstone wall, through the small stand of trees, to her childhood friend's back garden. A carpenter waved to her from his perch at the top of an aluminum ladder. His bare back glistened in the late-morning sun.

"They went to the beach," he shouted down.

"Thank you. Thanks a lot."

Krista turned back, again following the path back alongside the stone wall. She recalled the countless number of times over the years that Deirdre and she had stretched out the summer by going down to the water for just one more beach day. Each September, they prayed for more time, and then almost by magic or as if they had willed it to happen the late Indian summer would appear. They would be guaranteed another day or two of sunshine.

Sometimes it would amount to a whole week of golden days. No one really wanted to go off-Island, if there was another beach day to be had. No one wanted to go home for the winter.

Krista stopped walking and looked up at her bedroom window. Paint peeled from the gables, the shutters and the rusted drainpipe. The open drapes and half-lifted shade might make the casual passer-by believe someone actually lived there. She then looked across the path to the grey, weathered wooden door of the stable. She wished that Priscilla, the last of the horses to live there, a black Morgan Daddy Bourne bought her when she was sixteen, was still there. Krista imagined the horse waiting for her. She wanted to ride at a canter down the beach trail and walk along the waterline.

After Ilsa's death, the mare had been sent to Scrubby Neck Farm and Krista was not sure what had happened to her after that. She closed the green gate behind herself and took a long look at the garden, covered with fallen apples. Some had been on the ground for weeks, some a few days. She could gauge their age by their color: bright red, half green, yellow with decay. If Ilsa were still alive the grass would be cleared and trim and even as a carpet. My little golf course, she used to call it. The apples would have been raked up every day, before anyone else was awake to notice who it was that kept things so neat and orderly. Krista compared the lush ivy on the walls to the dry oak leaves, already falling to the ground.

Not really knowing why, she took the rake from against the garage door and the wheelbarrow from beside the compost pile. For a moment she pictured herself as a small girl helping her grandmother to pick up apples. She leaned the rake against the tree in readiness. Through its bare branches she caught a tantalizing glimpse of the sky and appraised it as she had learned to do over so many summers. It was a deep, unbroken china blue. Beach day, she decided, and left the apples to be raked later.

In the garage the car started instantly. Through its open windows she could hear the maples and oaks rustling to either side of the road. She drove quickly through Vineyard Haven, then Oak Bluffs. Passing the small firehouse, she glanced at the dark plate glass. Empty. *How many years had it been?* The sight of the squat little pepper-pot gazebo on the Edgartown Road pleased her as it always did. The shorefront houses were boarded up. The sea lashed the sea wall, spilling over here and there. At the Bend in the Road, an old favorite, she stopped and parked the car, leaving her sandals on the already sandy boards.

We used to swim here.

Krista thought of her grandmother delicately treading the narrow path through the dunes to the spot where grass, stiff and yellowing, waved in the sea breeze. From there the sand seemed to stretch away in infinitely graduated colors, all the way down to the waterline, where a border of seaweed lay drying in the sun. This was the time of year when Ilsa would haul back sacks of seaweed to mulch the garden. Krista walked down to where the sea met the shore.

Northern waters.

A tall ship was visible on the horizon, catching the wind in its sails and moving fast. Krista watched it. *A ghost from another time.* Nine knots, she guessed, recalling a sail she once took on an old twelve-gun sloop of war. The sand was warm. She sat down and rolled the legs of her grandmother's jeans up and over her shins. She wondered where Deirdre might be. *Would she have Justine with her?*

Krista had not seen her friend's little girl since she was born. The last summer the two friends had been here together, the one before Ilsa's death, when Krista had hidden by the walkway and listened to Deirdre's lament, Justine had been in Boston with her grandmother. Remembering that now, Krista wondered again about the fetus she had aborted. *My child would have been born in May. In May, will I think of the baby I chose not to have? Will I always count the missed birthdays?* With a sigh, she supposed that now and again she would. *Isn't it only natural to wonder how things might have turned out if I had made a different choice?*

A car braked on the far side of the dune. A man and a young child came running along the path. They nodded at Krista and turned left where she had turned right. A tiny red-and-orange float dangled from the end of the child's miniature fishing rod, keeping time with the dark silver weight dancing from the rod propped over the man's shoulder. They both had the same walk, the same blue jeans rolled up over the ankles.

Too cold to go in the water today.

Krista watched them walk down the beach together and choose a patch of the shoreline close to the water. The child was intent on being a fisherman, casting his short line out, never once grazing the water. His father stood behind him, patiently teaching him to cast, until the boy shrugged him off.

Krista lay back on the sand, ignoring the cool breeze that sought her out and tugged at her shirt and hair. With eyes closed, she pictured the pink floats that had marked off the swimming area – hauled in from the sea this late in the season. She remembered being proud of swimming with her thin, attractive grandmother as the two of them walked past the harassed mothers and their charges, left their towels neatly on dry sand, dropped their beach robes at the water's edge and walked right into the gentle surf. Krista recalled that it was Ilsa who had taught her to dive, go right beneath the waves, get her head wet and open her eyes only once she was back up at the surface.

Grandmother and grandchild would swim far out beyond the designated swimming area, then turn around and float back to shore. There they would sit on the sand for a few moments to take in the scene before toweling off and returning to the car. Ilsa would deftly untie her wet halter-neck suit and slip it off while still wearing the robe. They used to laugh about her knack for doing that and her habit of not bothering to put on underwear while she was still damp from the sea. It was yet another secret they loved to share. No one ever suspected that after swimming the Bourne girls shopped all but naked at the A&P, as well as the fruit stand on the highway.

Krista took a deep breath and sat up. There were many other places she wanted to revisit on the Island. She wanted to be grateful for everything: the Bend in the Road, the safe harbor, the toddler beach. Everything. Every moment of her childhood. What had happened, what had not. Of all the places she could think of at that moment, the destination that appealed to her the most was Lighthouse Beach.

Driving slowly through Edgartown, Krista admired the closely built houses along Main Street, their bright colors in the sun, their evenness and order. A few late roses blossomed on white picket fences. The courthouse was open; the sidewalks not yet emptied of tourists, though signs in shop windows already read: *See you next summer*.

She drove by the paper store, the Catholic church, the whaling church, the deli and the bank. Turning left at the drugstore, Krista remembered the candy store at the end of the next block. She parked by the long paved footpath that meandered its way to the wooden boardwalk. Looking at the harbor, she could recognize individual craft at their moorings. The fishing boats had unloaded their morning catch: the scent of it hung in the air, salty and alien. A yacht refueled. A guitar player strummed on the deck with a bilge pump for accompaniment. Krista walked unhurriedly towards the lighthouse.

No one swam in this water. She reminisced about the many times she'd visited this place with her father and the rare occasions when Helen had accompanied them. Her parents took one hand each and swung her off her feet at every third step, saying, "One, two, three... fly!" Several times she and her dad went to the lighthouse in the evening long after her normal bedtime. The moon was full. They stripped, then splashed in the low, incoming tide. She recalled the phosphorescence that she believed her father made just for her with the steady strokes of his arms as they powered through the water.

"It's a beach day," she said again, and understood that what she was really saying was: life is good. She undid the top buttons of her shirt.

Looking back towards the harbor, then the houses, restaurants and hotels bordering the front, she thought the scene resembled a beautiful tapestry. The autumn light was clear and golden, casting crisp-edged shadows. *This is better than any dream*, she decided, then wondered where Michael might be, knowing it would be impossible to track him down. She would have to wait for him to come back to the house, if he came back at all.

Letting one handful of sand after the next sift through her fingers, Krista felt free. She was not sure why. She dug her toes into the warm sand. She felt safe. At home. Stretching, straight-armed, out and over her toes, she felt her whole body elongate and then relax. *It feels great to be alive, right here, right now*, she realized.

Krista raced down to the water. She ran as far as the lighthouse and hopped onto the concrete plinth encircling it. Placing her hands on her hips she leaned back, looking up to the lantern room at the top, then across the harbor to Chappy, the point farthest out on the horizon. The air tasted so sweet she felt she might just bite into it. A beachcomber in a plaid jacket walked across the small bridge through the marsh hay further down the beach. Krista walked in his direction. They met the dead center of the sand.

"Do you have the time?" she asked.

"Noon," he answered, glancing at his watch, then up towards the Harbor View Hotel. "It's a shame they should want to build here," he added.

Krista looked in that direction. The ground had been leveled and marked off with string and red flags. The man continued on his way. The small pond under the bridge reflected the sky and the tall grasses bowing before the wind. Krista held on to the railing of the bridge, leaning all her weight in the other direction then pivoting round to switch hands on the railing and lean out again. This whole day, she decided, tasted as sweet and wholesome as an apple.

Krista leaned over the railing, changing her stretch. Then she threw one leg over it. She saw the reflection of her face in the water. For a split second the sight threw her off guard, then she laughed. *Not bad, considering. Not bad at all.* She swung the leg back over the rail, brought her ankles together and dismounted in a cushion *plié*. Walking gingerly off the bridge, she pretended to be on a high wire, placing one foot directly in front of the other.

Stepping off the bridge and into the sand, Krista noticed a small, furry black mound in the reeds with the water slowly lapping over it. A dead puppy lay in a fetal position, its eyes closed. Krista knelt beside the animal. She imagined the bitch that had carried it down to the sea. Had it been born dead? The tide would eventually take it. She noticed how the dog's body flattened out in the water. She wanted to walk away but could not.

Her stomach rumbled. The abortion seemed a lifetime ago. She recalled her reflection in the tidal pond. Her sorrow was immeasurable; her surrender deep. *I cannot bring you back.* Krista closed the reeds over the puppy. Looking out over the marsh, to the bridge, the shore and the horizon, she acknowledged her absolute powerlessness in the face of death.

She thought of all the things over which she had no control, all the things greater than herself. God. Winter. Rain. Sun. Earth. Sky. Other people. Then, for the first time, she gave thanks for the power she did have. *I said yes to something and I said no to something. I did think of myself and I thought of another. The decision had to be made. It didn't just happen to me.*

Krista understood her weakness and her courage, her fear and her bravery. She sensed that the boundary between right and wrong, and good and evil, was often indistinct. She sensed also that somehow, stumblingly, unconsciously, she had, for the first time in her adult life, made a commitment to do something and stuck by it. She idly watched the marsh hay dancing in the wind, recalling when the grasses had seemed to her like a dense, overwhelming jungle since she was not tall enough to see over their stems.

Walking back up the embankment to the asphalt road, she climbed over a steel gate half covered with swarming blackberry canes. The thought of the dead pup stirred her emotions again but this time it was not sadness she felt. It was compassion.

11

As Krista drove along Summer Street towards Main Street, she recognized St Andrew's, the small brick Anglican church she had sometimes attended with Ilsa. The funerals, Ilsa's and her father's, took place there. The processions, which had seemed interminably long, had then wound their way down Pease Point Way to the cemetery at its end. Identical striped canopies had sheltered each grave and the massive granite slab that bore great-great-grandfather Bourne's name at the top of the list dominated the family plots. Other names were chiseled below his, as on a war memorial. The patriarch had bought a large enough site for ten generations. At the moment it looked as though Krista's would be the last.

Some impulse directed her to park the car. She found a space in front of the doctor's office directly across from the small church.

I will only be a minute. Just a short prayer. I want to bury my dead. Don't I owe her... him... that much?

The building seemed smaller than she remembered. Outside, a painted iron sign read *Open for Prayer and*

Meditation. Adjacent to the church, the pastor's door stood ajar. Krista was almost tempted to go in and seek him out. Instead, she stepped into the church. Inside it appeared positively diminutive. Krista could not recall the church being so small before or herself feeling so large. The feeling brought to mind a drawing she had seen in an edition of *Alice in Wonderland* years ago: Alice's neck bent under the weight of the ceiling.

Daylight filtered through the stained-glass windows to either side and behind the altar. It felt cooler in here than it had in the fall sunshine outside. Krista chose to sit. *Take a rest.* Her eyes and ears adjusted to the church's interior. She noticed someone busying herself around the pulpit, elaborately carved to resemble the prow of a boat. It always drew her attention during every service and each funeral. *Sailing away.*

From her seat on the back pew, Krista leaned back against the paneled wall. She thumbed through a hymnal and the *Book of Common Prayer*, drawing comfort from its familiarity.

"May I help you?" the white-haired woman asked as she descended from the pulpit.

"I'm here to reflect," Krista told her, and the woman nodded her head in understanding and left her to it, while she herself went to the front of the church, lifting red cushions off the pews in the choir stall then busily shaking and replacing them. The church's interior smelled of furniture polish, wax, flowers and the sea breeze.

Krista touched the wooden seat beneath her. *When was the last time I was in church? For Ilsa's funeral?* She and Michael had gone to a church on Park Avenue one Saturday, just for fun. She had asked him if he could guess her religion.

"Anglican?"

"No."

"No?"

"No. I believe in the planets spinning in their fields of gravity all around the sun, electrons dancing around a nucleus, you around me."

"What about *you around me*?"

Then Krista remembered the last time she had been in church. It was Easter at Riverside Church. There had been a trumpet fanfare and afterwards a full orchestra playing; Reverend Coffin and six hundred men – men of the ages, they were called – carved into the walls. The face of Hippocrates graced the panel dedicated to science, as did Einstein's. Helen had taken her there in one of her increasingly random attempts at motherhood. Krista could not help smiling at the memory. It had been a good performance, if not entirely successful. Afterwards they discussed the service, the building, the rector, over lunch in a restaurant with pink tablecloths. They might just as well have been to a Broadway show.

Krista felt the gratitude she'd experienced earlier extending even as far as her mother, the one woman she had come close to believing she hated. In that moment Krista wished Helen were with her. She wanted her to say something, even if it were only a suggestion that her daughter read this or that. She pictured Helen admonishing her, as she gulped freshly squeezed orange juice, popped a multivitamin, got ready to run to another class, a seminar, a meeting with an editor.

"Kris, don't sweat it. You made a decision. Good for you."

Then she would return to the old, old theme.

"You had a choice. Imagine how it was for me. At your age, I had no choice. Try imagining no choice."

Krista could not fathom not having a choice. She sighed, leaned forward and rested her forehead on the back of the pew in front of her. *It is not the decision I regret. It is this feeling of death, of loss.* She let her thoughts wander, and her eyes roam over the brick walls, the Stations of the Cross, the American flag, the black numerals on the board for the hymns sung last week. She stood up. There was nothing here that could bring back…

Krista could not finish her thought. *What is it? What do I want to bring back?* Looking up at the floor-to-ceiling pipes of the organ, she asked herself again and again: *What is it? Not my father. Not the glitter I once saw on the ceiling.*

Her eyes filmed over with tears. *What am I doing here? What do I want? Forgiveness? Mercy? For what?* She straightened her spine, feeling like a defendant awaiting sentence.

She imagined her mother again, giving judgment.

"You made a decision – with your own best interest at heart."

Krista felt herself caught up in a sort of perpetual twilight. She felt like the last person at a wake. Even the body of the dead had been carted off.

Is my crime, my sin, not about an unborn child at all but a denial of myself and life as it might have unfolded for me?

Krista did not know and realized it was unknowable.

I will never know the outcome of a choice I did not make. And for that I am sincerely sorry.

The white-haired woman was busily searching for something, Krista belatedly realized. She walked up the aisle.

"What are you looking for?"

"Some notes."

"Notes?"

"For a sermon."

"Do you want some help?"

The woman beamed at her with gratitude.

"That would be very kind of you."

Krista began the hunt, searching the prow of the pulpit a second time and under cushions. Amazingly, she found the index cards, perched on the corner of the linen-covered altar.

"My eyes, they just don't work like they used to," the woman told her apologetically. They were bright and blue, friendly-looking.

"They were hidden in plain sight," Krista told her. "White on white. That's tough for anyone to see."

"Well, thank you so much for finding them. I have a reconciliation to perform shortly and I wouldn't want to do it without these."

"Are you a priest?"

"Yes."

"Ordained?"

The woman smiled at her, obviously used to explaining. "It's not so unusual, you know. I was ordained in 1978."

"I'm surprised."

"By what?"

"The fact that you're a priest."

The woman started to excuse herself, obviously eager to prepare for the ceremony.

"No, wait. What is a reconciliation?" Krista asked.

"An act of forgiveness."

"For what?"

"Any transgression."

Again she turned to leave.

"Please, wait," Krista whispered. "I think this might be important for me."

The priest looked directly at her.

"What if you haven't transgressed, or sinned, or whatever?" asked Krista. "Or, at least, you're told that you have not."

"Then," the woman laughed, "you're canonized."

Where do I begin? No, better not try to explain, Krista decided.

"What if you just want peace? What if what you chose to do was not against the law, but still you felt pain and remorse? And also loss," she continued. "My father died sixteen years ago. My grandmother eighteen months ago."

"I see. Well, bereavement can be—"

"It's not just their deaths. It's my abortion too," Krista told her, making up her mind to tell it all to this woman with her kindly eyes.

"Sit down here for a moment," the priest told her and led the way.

They sat together on the altar step. Krista looked down at the carpet rather than meet those frank blue eyes. It would be unbearable to see any change in them after her admission.

"Do you think it was a sin?" the priest queried, keeping her voice low and averting her face slightly so that anyone who happened to come into the church would not realize the significance of this discussion.

"No," Krista answered immediately. "I mean… I don't know. I hurt. *It* hurt me incredibly, and I could have had the child." The priest crossed her leg towards Krista, brushing the hem of her poplin skirt. Krista looked out at the sunlight beyond the wide-open door. "I knew the minute I conceived. I asked for it. I didn't really believe I had that power. Do you know what I mean?"

"You weren't ready," was the soothing response. "You look very young still."

"No, I wasn't ready for a baby, the pain, any of it," she agreed. "But I'm not asking for forgiveness."

"I know. You want peace."

Krista wanted to run. She wanted to be on the bridge overlooking the marsh again. "The abortion was the first right decision I ever made. I don't think I even made a decision before that. I thought it was the right thing to do, but it caused pain to more than one person. I felt a life taken from me. At its beginning there was this white, searing sort of light."

The priest nodded.

"Other women have told me the same thing."

"But no one told me! I didn't know, I really didn't. And no one warned me about the pain."

"Incredible, isn't it?" the priest said. "And it's not something most women talk about."

Krista frowned.

"But why don't they?"

"From fear, I expect. Because what does pain imply? Guilt, punishment, some sort of wrongdoing. Some women can't verbalize the pain, and others are afraid it might fuel the argument that abortion is unlawful. They think only preserving silence will protect their right to choose."

Krista considered this for a while.

"Growing up," she said, "is a challenge. Recognizing the power you have to shape your own life, and the responsibility that brings with it."

Inside the church everything was still, expectant. The sounds of everyday life being conducted outside filled the vacuum. A lawnmower droned in the distance. Pigeons crooned throatily and made occasional desperate-sounding flurries in the eaves outside. Someone honked impatiently, caught by the stop sign just yards from the door.

"I have a sense of being a different person since the abortion," Krista confided.

"How are you different?"

"I have a better understanding of love, maybe. And compassion. I don't understand how a decision I thought was so right could turn out to have caused so much hurt. It changed me. I felt terror, death, loss, like never before. But today on the beach I felt joy. Deep, unalloyed joy."

The frown line between the priest's eyes eased slightly. "That's good to hear. God has blessed you. If you've found joy, peace cannot be far off."

"What about forgiveness?"

"For what?"

"Not for taking life but for being careless with it. I think, before this, I was living my life carelessly."

The priest lifted the bifocals that dangled from a chain about her neck and put them on. Her magnified eyes studied Krista closely for a moment: the graceful lines of her long limbs, tangled mass of hair, clothes that seemed fit only for the trash. The sweetness and seriousness of youth.

"You're forgiven, my dear, when you can forgive yourself," her confessor told her.

Krista's shoulders twitched. She could feel the burden under which she had labored easing and slipping away.

"I am so sorry to have kept you," she murmured.

"Heavens, don't be! It's what I'm here for. And I have a few minutes yet."

"Thank you," Krista told her as they walked to the door together.

"Take care of yourself," the priest said as they parted.

"I will, but don't I have to do something first? I mean, penance of some kind?"

"Oh, yes. I know... your penance is to tell someone you know about this. The pain and what you learnt from it."

Outside in the radiant afternoon Krista guessed the priest's reconciliation service would be running late until she noticed the arrival of a middle-aged man. He strode purposefully up the path, smiling and tipping his black cap with its Red Ball insignia to her as he stepped past her into the church. Krista stood with her hands thrust into the pockets of her grandmother's jeans. Her loose shirt tails flapped in the breeze. She marveled at everything. The weather, the church, the man going in to unburden himself of his pain. Life. But most of all the infinite capacity of the human heart to learn and to love.

12

For the second time that day Krista thought of Priscilla, the old Morgan. How many times had she passed the horse crossing sign on the West Tisbury Road? *Hundreds.* Instead of returning to the house to close up, she took a left off the highway. She felt she must drive to Scrubby Neck Farm. She had a premonition. She thought there might be a chance, albeit a slim one, that the stable owner would still have Priscilla. Krista also wanted to take in the beach trail in the same way she had taken in the Bend in the Road and Lighthouse Beach. She wanted to look back, before looking ahead.

The black Morgan was still at the farm.

"Best trail horse we have," the manager said. "Take her." He handed Krista the tack. "Looks like she must know you, just a little." He laughed as Priscilla nodded vigorously in her box, pawing the sawdust.

"Thank you, thank you, thank you." Krista nearly kissed the old man.

She slipped off the horse's halter.

"Just have her back by four. I have riders coming in then." He paused and studied her ragbag clothes. "If you want those boots in the tack room, use them."

"No problem. She will be back in good time."

Krista left the barn and walked the horse under a canopy of oaks. They rode towards Watcha Path. Everything appeared familiar yet brand new. Again, Krista felt as if she were biting into a fresh red apple. She gripped the horse gently with the insides of her thighs and calves. Priscilla, with her ears pricked forward, fell into an easy, familiar rhythm.

$$\sim$$

Krista reined the old Morgan to the left, where the tall encroaching oaks gave way to scrub and the shoreline woods opened up. Krista savored the sight of the low, rolling terrain, the landscape she knew so well. Earth crumbled away underfoot as they picked their way, crab-like, down the side of a gully.

At the far side of the ditch, Krista and Priscilla crossed a meadow towards a forest of pine. Breaking off a grass head, Krista inhaled deeply before tossing it over her shoulder.

"First I must forgive myself," she said against the sound of the sea roaring in the distance and the breeze setting the pines sighing.

Forgiveness. What was that exactly? Krista felt that there was something the priest had left unsaid. She descended into a cool hollow spiced with the scent of bayberry. Long Point Cove rose up over the next hill. In the pine grove, Krista patted the side of the mare's neck.

She barely tapped her with her heels and Priscilla broke into a canter, scattering a trio of blue jays.

I cannot forgive myself.

The horse stumbled and Krista brought her to a halt.

How do I forgive myself?

"By forgiving others."

Krista looked around. It was her grandmother's voice again.

"Ilsa?"

The sound of the breaking waves intensified.

Forgive others? Who?

"Stop cutting people out of your life."

But who? Helen. Michael. My father. Yes, even him. In all my searching, all my daydreaming, I never once allowed him to be who he truly was. I hated him for his disappearance. I did cut him out.

"Krista, you cut everyone out."

"How, Ilsa? Please tell me," she said aloud.

"By not being yourself."

Clusters of goldenrod and wild carrot bordered the trail. Rider and horse approached Long Point Cove. Priscilla stepped gingerly around the shrubby vegetation. *Cutting off, cutting out. That is how I deal with pain.* Krista thought of the previous day when she had wanted to die.

"Okay," she said, "I forgive..."

The horse tugged at the reins.

"... anyone who ever asked it of me."

Priscilla eased herself into a trot.

"And myself. I forgive myself."

I accept myself.

Krista realized she wanted to see Michael again. *I want to go home.* The path wound its way alongside the pond, through low-lying grasses and past an otter trail to the dunes. *If I learn to forgive others, I can forgive myself. If I learn to accept myself, I can accept others.*

"Priscilla," she said to her old friend, "I am not sure how this all works but I am getting there."

Krista listened to the mare's steady breathing, drawing deeply into the wind off the ocean. *I forgive myself for my carelessness. For taking life for granted.*

"I forgive myself," she said aloud.

Beyond the dunes the haze rose off the horizon. Thundering surf shattered her reverie. Priscilla drank from a freshwater pond. The wind picked up. The grasses parted to reveal the rosehips waiting to be harvested.

The sea churned and the sun cast its light across the Atlantic like a net. Krista kept the horse still while she drank in the sight. *This is better than any dream, better than any longing for what I do not have,* she realized. She urged Priscilla into a canter, splashing through the sea grass and sidestepping a late blooming butter 'n' eggs. *We come of age when we come of age.* As she rode through the shimmering marsh hay, Krista remembered Ilsa's iridescent landscapes. *Her inspiration was not so hard to find.* Then she rode without thinking, drawing in great drafts of fresh autumn air as if she had just learned to breathe.

Priscilla broke into a lather. Krista dismounted and led the horse over to the lee of a small hill. She saw two figures sunbathing in the distance, and recognized

Deirdre. A small child in a swimsuit played with a bucket, spilling seashells onto the sand. For a moment Krista felt frightened of approaching her old friend.

She will know.

I forgive… I forgive myself.

Deirdre spotted her and windmilled her arms around. Her hair, darkened from its childhood blondness, lifted in the breeze. Her short cotton dress billowed.

"Kris!" She ran towards horse and rider. "I can't believe it's you."

"It's me. Though I can't believe it either," said Krista, sliding from the saddle. The two women kissed.

"Just last night I was thinking about you – that it was a shame your house was empty." Deidre hugged her friend and turned towards her daughter, "Look, Justine. This is Mother's friend, from when we were babies."

Krista smiled and knelt before the small child, who seemed impressed only with the black Morgan, who was only impressed with the grass. The two women sat on a piece of driftwood. While Krista loosely tied Priscilla's reins to the branch end of the bleached log, she watched Deidre persuade her little girl to pull on a sundress over her swimsuit and a floppy-brimmed hat. Tired of the horse, she had returned to placing mussel shells around a mound of sand.

"What are you doing on Priscilla?" asked Deidre.

"Riding."

"No! I mean, what are you doing here?"

"Came in search of some ocean air. On the seven o'clock boat."

Krista carefully didn't say which day.

"This morning?" Deidre asked, and Krista crossed her fingers.

"Yes, this morning."

"Why didn't you come over to the house?"

"I did. Your carpenter said you went to the beach."

"We're leaving today," Deidre said, pulling a face. "We were going to go earlier, but when the mist burned off, I just knew it would be a beach day."

"It can't last forever," Krista said. They both laughed, and watched Justine embellish her castle.

"So this is just time out for you?" asked Deidre.

"Not exactly."

Deidre looked closely at her friend. "Then what is it exactly?"

"I had an abortion."

"Kris! I am so sorry."

"Afterwards I ran away. It was so painful, I felt as if my insides had been ripped out. I wanted to die."

"I know," said Deirdre. "I had one two years ago, around this time of year. In fact, just now – funny – I was thinking about that baby. How old it would be if I'd… But I had to do it, Krista. Can you imagine? Unmarried, with *two* children?"

Justine poured buckets of dry sand over her castle. She then ran to retrieve a plastic shovel from beside the wicker picnic basket, asking Deirdre for an orange simultaneously. A low-flying helicopter on the horizon startled her. She dropped her fruit instantly and tried desperately to shelter between her mother's knees. Deirdre embraced her, lowering her own head, looking up from under her brow at the Coast Guard helicopter.

"She hates those things. They fly low all the time. She always panics," Deidre explained to Krista.

The child sheltered behind her mother's comforting arms until the helicopter receded down the beach. Then she returned to her sandy fortress.

"I wonder what to teach her when she comes of age," Deidre mused aloud. "About abortion."

"She should know about the pain."

"It's not knowable."

"Yes, but there should at least be some sort of warning. They do it for cigarettes."

"But it's unknowable until it happens to you. With both her birth and the abortion, I didn't know – I couldn't have known – until they happened."

"I still think a warning…"

"Don't you think anyone did?"

"No."

"Maybe you didn't hear it. With your mother, there wasn't anything that wasn't discussed."

"It didn't register with me before this that I am capable of creating life. That sex leads to that."

"It all starts before we know which end is up."

"I actually asked for it. Life. Then there was this sort of white heat, like a light flipping on."

"Me too, both times!"

"They ought to put *that* in a manual."

Krista's voice trailed off. She was thinking about *My Body, My Body*.

"You won't believe what else I did."

"What?"

"I burnt all Helen's books!"

"You didn't!"

"I did."

"What did she say?"

"I don't know, I haven't spoken with her since."

Krista rolled up her jeans and took off her riding boots. Deirdre looked longingly at Priscilla.

"Do you think I could take her for a ride?"

"Of course. Not for too long, though. Priscilla needs to be back by four."

"Righto," Deirdre answered. She yanked on the boots then trotted off on the Morgan along the private beach.

13

The little girl walked towards Krista. She stood and watched her mother canter up the ridge above the pond.

"Momma – where'd she go?"

The child looked at Krista. Her lower lip quivered. She turned right and left as if looking for a pair of knees to hide between.

"Come on, Justine."

Krista walked towards a dune scattered with mussel shells. Sandpipers scurried at the edge of the surf. Gulls lifted and landed. Justine skittered when a low-flying bird brushed too close. Krista continued to talk, not giving the child a chance to cry.

"What are these?" she asked.

"Shells," the little girl answered confidently.

"If we put two together," Krista rearranged the shells, "we have butterflies – butterflies to protect the castle. A legion of Monarchs."

The child crouched down, intent on making butterflies.
"Butterfly."

Krista found a stick, a handful of shells, a piece of coral and a blue jay feather. The child emulated her every move, placing objects the exact same way. Across the top of the dune Krista carved a path with a stick and placed a column of mussel shells in pairs upon it. She poked the feather into the sand at the far end of the column. It stirred in the breeze, giving the impression that the line of shells was a string of wings ready for take-off. Justine handed Krista a crab shell with one claw still intact. They placed it in the column. White stones were placed in a double file.

"This is the path to the castle," Krista said.

"Road," Justine corrected her.

"Yes, of course. Road."

"Stone."

Krista guided Justine in and out of fantasy. The make-believe castle had its own guard made up of butterflies. A stick king and queen. An army of pirates. Justine followed Krista's lead. Then piece by piece they took the castle apart, tossing a butterfly here or there, calling it a seashell. They scattered the stones in every direction.

"No road," said Justine finally, as eager to dismantle the castle as she had been to build it. Taking a long stick, she pressed the surface of the dune smooth again. Something made her stop. Looking at Krista, she said nothing but cocked an ear. Down the beach, a low-flying plane made its appearance. The child panicked, attempting to climb between Krista's knees. Without thinking, Krista embraced her as she had seen Deirdre do.

Surprised by the child's fear, Krista watched the plane approach, trying to perceive it as Justine might. While she tried the child's fear on for size, Krista reflected on her own fear. *Fear of living.* That, she thought, was what she most needed to forgive herself for – fear of living.

"Justine," she said, "it's just an airplane."

"Airplane."

"Airplane. Look, there's a man inside. Wave!"

Justine stood very still. Krista waved for both of them.

"Look," she said again.

The pilot waved back at them. Justine surfaced from between Krista's knees. Stepping out, she placed her hands on her hips and watched in amazement until the airplane disappeared. Then she got back to demolishing the castle.

"Castle gone," she said finally as she put down the stick and brushed the sand from her hands.

"Castle gone," Krista confirmed.

"Walk?" the child asked, pointing in the direction in which the plane had gone.

They held hands and began a stroll down the empty beach. Another helicopter clattered in the distance. Justine grabbed Krista's legs, demanding to be picked up. Krista ignored this.

"Flying man," she told her, "there's a man flying. Wave!"

Krista waved in a broad arc but Justine paid no attention. Instead, she pressed her face tight against Krista's leg until the helicopter was directly overhead.

"Look," Krista told her. "He's waving to you."

"To me?"

"To you."

Justine pulled away from Krista's legs and waved at the helicopter until it was well out of sight. They resumed their walk, with the child once again cowering at the sight of a seagull shadow crossing her path.

"Look at this," Krista said to her. "Justine, look at me."

The little girl paid quiet attention. With outstretched arms, Krista cast a bird-like shadow over the sand.

"Fly," she demanded of the little one. "Hold out your arms like this."

The child indignantly refused. Instead she ran holding her fat little arms folded tightly over her chest. For a moment Krista remembered herself flying helplessly in her dream, arms crossed over her heart. She caught Justine from behind, directing her attention to a seabird flying overhead.

"Look at that," she said. "Look at the bird. Flying. Like the man in the plane."

She set the child down.

"Fly!" Krista invited the child again.

Instead, Justine merely ran behind Krista, hiding in her shadow whenever a bird passed overhead. Krista watched the child watching the shadow in flight. She tossed up her arms once in a small experiment before quickly restoring them to her sides. Then she placed Justine on her shoulders and held her arms straight out with her own.

"Look," she said. "Our shadow has wings!"

Krista flapped her arms. Justine left hers extended, perfectly balanced, not afraid of falling. Another gull passed overhead. It landed and broke out in raucous cries. Further up the beach and at a greater altitude than the previous aircraft, a biplane flew past silently.

"Look, Justine. A wing on top of a wing. Like you and me!"

The toddler arched her back, holding tightly to Krista's hands, and screeched with delight. They flapped their wings in unison, casting shadows upon the sand. To anyone else they might be any mother and child playing together on a late beach day. Krista brought Justine back to the ground and the child noticed her own shadow. She tossed up her arms.

"Flying!" she cried.

Justine brought her chubby knees to her chest and jumped. She outdistanced Krista until, from behind, Krista finally swooped down and caught the child under her arms before spinning her around in great circles.

"Follow me," Justine ordered, "fly, fly, fly."

Suddenly, Krista realized they had traveled quite a distance from the spot where they had built the sandcastle. She instantly turned the little girl around and marched back up the beach. Priscilla would have to be back soon. In the about-face, the shadows disappeared. They no longer fell in front, but behind. Justine halted to stare at them, as if feeling astonished or cheated.

"Where did the shadows go?" asked Krista, guessing her thoughts.

The child did not answer and Krista mimed a search. She looked behind herself, in the pockets of her jeans. Justine did the same and then hid behind her mother's friend. The game turned to one of peek-a-boo.

"Where did Justine go?"

"Here," the child called out, as she ran from behind, "me not gone."

Justine wrapped her arms around Krista's legs. They laughed together joyously. Krista watched as Justine threw up her arms, flying ahead – no longer needing a shadow. Krista ran past her, turned and picked her up. They spun, both squealing with delight. They copied one another. First, they took little steps, then big ones, and finally they discovered their own footprints leading down the beach. Justine stepped into the footprints that were her own. They scoured the ground, looking for discarded treasures. Justine planted her feet into Krista's old footprints.

"Whose feet now?"

"You tell me," Krista urged.

"Giant feet," Justine answered.

She was so intent on the oversized footprints that she walked into the breaking surf. Water splashed across her chest. Retrieving her quickly, Krista spun her around and quickly set her back in her own small prints, though now these were mostly washed away by the incoming tide. Finally Krista swept up the child and held her against her chest. The toddler wrapped her chubby legs around Krista's back. Her heart beat against Krista's.

"Where did the baby go?" Krista asked.

Justine rested for a moment with her head tucked under Krista's chin. She looked down at the small footprints filling with water, almost erased. She looked at Krista, then arched herself up and back. She pointed directly overhead.

"Into the sun," she squealed.

"Into the sun." Krista smiled.

14

Deirdre and Krista hugged. Each promised to visit the other soon. In Boston or New York. They made this same pledge year after year at the end of the season, but seldom saw each other except in the summer. Deirdre packed her beach bag and her wicker hamper. Justine ran around the two women, holding her beach towel over her head, trying to see its shadow, which disappeared whenever she stopped to look for it. Under her breath, she hummed to herself.

"Running, Mommy, running. Flying, Mommy, flying."

Deirdre picked her daughter up and placed her on her hip.

"Say goodbye."

The child looked up at Krista. For an instant she snuggled deeper into her mother's chest, then loudly demanded her seashells. Deirdre set her down, and pulled out a plastic bag full of white scallop and dark-blue mussel shells. The child reached into the clear bag, extracting precisely two of her treasures. She handed one to Krista and curled the other up in a tight little fist held against her chest.

"Well, I am impressed with you, young lady," Deirdre said, putting the bag of treasures back into the tote, "you must be nearly three." She looked at Krista, half whispering, "That's when they learn to give."

"Thank you, Justine. I will treasure it forever," Krista told her.

She mounted Priscilla and started off down the beach, Deirdre waving goodbye until it was time to catch and subdue Justine who, with her small towel flying behind her, could not seem to get enough of flying.

With the horse delivered back to Scrubby Neck, Krista drove to the house. As she parked, she realized she was not ready to leave. She calculated that she could take the last boat, the ten o'clock ferry. In the house, she found her half-nibbled bar of chocolate. She tasted a piece. Despite the warm day, the house was still cold, and just as she had gone down to the shore for the last beach day, now she went into the backyard to enjoy the last minutes of sunshine. After rinsing the shell Justine had given her and setting it to dry on the flat stone under the drainpipe, Krista reminded herself not to forget it. She wanted to take it home. To give to Michael, she thought idly.

Picking up the rake, she began to comb through the grass for fallen apples. When she had a pile, Krista began tossing one after the next into the wheelbarrow. By the sound of the plunk they made, she knew whether she hit the bottom, the side or entirely missed the wheelbarrow. The dead grass she raked into armfuls and tossed into the wheelbarrow as well. She sat down briefly on the grass and studied Ilsa's neglected garden. The coral-bells were still in bloom, the Shasta daisies seemed to shout out for attention, and the dark elephant ears were only now beginning to turn yellow. She looked at the Rose of Sharon, which Ilsa had always struggled to prevent its spreading. The apple tree, the young maple and the ivy covering the wall that enclosed the yard, all seemed to embrace her.

Krista lay back on the soft grass and closed her eyes. She felt content to be here. *At just this time of year, at this point in my life.* She took a deep breath.

She heard a car turn into the driveway. Michael had come to her. She stood up and reached for the rake while she watched him approach. He stood under the brick arch awaiting her reaction.

"Hi, stranger," he said warily.

"Hi, yourself," she answered.

"What are you doing?" he asked awkwardly.

"What does it look like I'm doing?"

"Leaning on a rake?"

"Picking up apples."

"Why?"

"Because I want to."

Krista picked up the fallen fruit and continued bundling up the long grass.

"Don't just stand there," she said. "Come and help me."

Michael entered the garden, knelt and began to pick up apples.

"Into the wheelbarrow," she said over her shoulder.

For a few minutes they worked in silence.

"How do you feel?" he asked her.

"Hungry."

"Good. I was worried about you. So is Helen, by the way."

Krista tossed another bundle of grass into the wheelbarrow.

"Call her. She's your mother."

"I'll see her tonight."

"All right," he said, throwing apples into the center of the lawn.

"In the wheelbarrow," Krista directed him. "Or if you can toss that far, behind the maple and into the compost."

"They're biodegradable. Leave them where they are."

They fell silent again, each keeping to their task until the lawn was finally clear of apples.

"How's D.B.?" she asked.

"Okay. Not worried at all. Said you probably came here and that you'd be back."

"You should have listened to him." She paused, leaning on the rake. "So what really brought you here, Michael? I thought you were through with me."

"I got halfway to Newark before I realized you were lying. I figured, if money didn't matter before, why should it matter now?"

Krista laughed. "You are so—"

"Stupid?" he answered.

"No."

"On the ferry, I heard someone say 'Hey, stupid' and I turned around. I thought they were talking to me."

Michael looked at the apple in his hand and turned it over. Krista walked up close to him and brushed the hair away from his forehead.

"Anyone ever tell you, you ride a good race?"

"Yes," he said, aiming the apple to the far side of the maple and hitting the compost. "A blond I met a long time ago."

A telephone rang. They turned simultaneously to the house and the open screen door. Krista chose to ignore the phone and returned to raking. Michael pulled the rake from her hands.

"Answer it," he said.

"No." She took the rake back.

"If you won't, I will."

Krista shrugged her shoulders and Michael made for the house.

"You are a child," he called back to her. "I am going to tell her you are here, out of your mind."

Krista stood for a moment before throwing the rake down. She met Michael in the study by the telephone.

"Here," he said, "it's your mother calling."

"Fine." Krista listened for a moment, frowning and pulling a face. "No, I didn't tell you because I didn't think about it," she said into the receiver.

She chose her words carefully. She wanted them to sting. *Forgive. I must forgive. I must forgive others and myself*, she remembered then.

"Hurt?" she repeated incredulously. "You're asking me did it hurt?"

She looked at Michael while she spoke to her mother.

"Yes, Helen, it hurt. I wish you, or someone else, anyone, would have told me the truth – how much it hurt. Why didn't they put that in the book?"

Then she cried into the phone.

"Yes," she said finally, collecting herself, "tonight."

Krista hung up, walked back outside and picked up the rake. Michael followed her out, turning her gently around and lifting her hair back over her shoulders.

"I'm sorry," he whispered, cradling her against his chest.

"Me, too. I am so sorry." And she cried as she had never cried before.

When the sobbing subsided, Krista listened to Michael's heart. She looked up and she kissed him. *As if it were the first time.* He cried.

"You're not supposed to do that," she said.

"I know."

They stepped away from each other and tended to the last two piles of apples.

"Michael," Krista finally called out, as she lifted a single apple, rocking it precariously forward and backward, "would you like a bite?"

"A bite?" he said, stopping momentarily, then playfully knocking her to the ground. "I want the whole thing."

"No," she said, pushing him away, "not for six weeks. Isn't that what Blackwell said?"

"No kissing for six weeks?"

They wrestled. Krista pretended to escape. He insisted on capturing her. They rolled on the ground and laughed at the work undone.

"You are beautiful," he said to her as he lifted himself up on one arm, "even more so than I remember." He lay back, looking at the sky through the uppermost branches of the apple tree.

"Thanks," she said as she got to her feet and pushed the wheelbarrow back to the compost pile before turning it over.

"I'm serious."

"I know. I am, too. Thank you."

Krista returned the rake to the shed behind the kitchen. The screen door slammed.

"Come on," she called out to Michael, still lying on the ground with his elbows cocked and hands behind his head. "Let's close up."

"You're ready to leave?"

"Yes," she answered, closing the shutters. "Time to go off-Island."

"I was just beginning to like it here," he said, coming through the kitchen, closing the basement door.

"Close the upstairs windows, will you? And do something with the spread in the back room."

"Like what?"

"Throw it out."

They busied themselves, locking up, closing the house. Together they draped the piano in the dining room. They closed the cupboards in the kitchen and turned off the stove, which did nothing anyway to warm the house against drafts.

"Kris," Michael asked, carrying an old stack of newspapers from the study to the kitchen, "what are you going to do now?"

"About what?"

"Back in the City."

Krista poked the dust rag she had used earlier back into the shopping bag on the cellar door.

"I'm going to dance," she answered. "I am going to find myself another teacher and dance."

They double-checked doors and windows and left through the kitchen. In the driveway they decided who would lead and who would follow, regretting that they each had their own car. Michael stepped into his and started the engine.

"No, wait," Krista called out, quickly getting out of her car and knocking on his window, "come with me."

"Okay."

"I forgot something."

She hurried behind the house, through the cellar door, up the basement steps, through the dining room, the study, the foyer, up the front stairs and into Ilsa's studio. She threw things out of the top of the small blue cabinet, finally finding the straw basket that contained Ilsa's sewing kit. She took the spool of gold thread and broke off a piece. Again, she ran through the house, stopping in the room behind the kitchen to pick up the hammer hanging beside the builder's angle. She opened the toolbox and picked out an awl.

"Just a minute." She smiled at Michael as she knelt in the garden.

"What are you doing?"

"You'll see."

She retrieved the dry white shell Justine had given her earlier that day from the flat stone under the drainpipe. As she stooped to pick it up, she hesitated for a moment, flooded with memories of another shell placed there many years ago the morning her father had disappeared forever. A breeze rustled the ivy, the tree and the border of elephant ears. It seemed to pass down the brick path between the house and the garage and vanish through the vine-covered arbor.

Krista turned the shell over. She angled the steel awl and knocked a perfectly formed hole through the ridged whiteness as Ilsa had taught her. *Into the sun.* She recalled Justine's voice as she picked up the gold thread, folded it in half and slipped it through the hole. Pulling the double ends of the thread through the loop, she let the shell dangle as they did on Ilsa's Christmas tree. It spiraled beneath her fingers and she handed it to Michael.

"Thank you," he said.

"You're welcome," she answered. "Keep it safe until we get home."

ABOUT THE AUTHOR

Marlene Hauser is a professional writer based in Oxford, UK, where she lives with her husband and teenage son. She served as editor of the *Writer's New York City Source Book* and originated the television film *Under the Influence*, going on to serve as Associate Producer and Technical Consultant. She holds an MFA in Creative Writing from Columbia University.